Stephen C. Challis

Cruel is the Snow

Revised Edition

Cruel is the Snow

(That sweeps Glencoe)
<u>Revised Edition</u>

This book is written in British English spelling.

Laird Stephen C. Challis

CRUEL IS THE SNOW

First edition. February 15, 2024.

ISBN: 979-8989961979

Written by Stephen C. Challis.

Table of Contents

Dedication

<u>*The Ballard of Glencoe Jim McClean 1963*</u>

Oh, cruel is the snow that sweeps Glencoe
And covers the grave o' Donald;
Oh, cruel was the foe that raped Glencoe
And murdered the house of MacDonald.
They came in the blizzard; we offered them heat,
A roof for their heads, dry shoes for their feet;
We wined them and dined them; they ate of our meat,
And they slept in the house of MacDonald
They came from Fort William with murder in mind;
The Campbell had orders King William had signed;
"Put all to the sword," these words underlined,
"And leave none alive called MacDonald."
They came in the night when the men were asleep,
This band of Argyles, through snow soft and deep;
Like murdering foxes amongst helpless sheep,
They slaughtered the house of MacDonald.
Some died in their beds at the hand o the foe;
Some fled in the night and were lost in the snow;
Some lived to accuse him what struck the first blow.
But gone was the house of MacDonald.

Dedication

This book is dedicated to the 38 innocent victims of the Massacre of Glencoe. They were murdered in their homes early on the morning of the 13th of February, 1692, by a detachment of British Troops under the command of Captain Robert Campbell, of Glenlyon; who had been the guests of their victims for 2 weeks?

CRUEL IS THE SNOW

Acknowledgements

The author wishes to acknowledge the following persons and books used in researching Cruel is the Snow.

Harold Temperley: The Revolution and the Revolution settlement in Great Britain (1687 – 1702)

C. Gifilan: Massacre of Glencoe of 1692, Brittanica.Com

BBC History of Scotland

The Scotsman

John Sadler: The Massacre of Glencoe

Glencoe Massacre visitors' centre, Inverness

Donald McBane: The Master Swordsman

Trip Advisor: Undiscovered Scotland.Co.Uk

Heritage Ireland

W.burntpit.com

Eva Challis

Prologue

It was a fine, calm morning in the summer of 1977 when we left the small fishing village of Ballachulish, Glencoe, Scotland. I had hired a small clinker built skiff and headed out across the mirror-like waters of Loch Leven. Our destination was the small island of Eilean Munde, just a short distance offshore.

We had been at Glencoe for three days on a camping holiday. While there, we had heard for the first time, about the massacre of the inhabitants of the village in the year 1692 by the British redcoats, under circumstances that still cause great divisions among the MacDonald and Campbell clans to this day.

The locals informed us that they had buried the Chief of the clan, who was murdered that night, on the Island. There were two fellow campers along with me in the boat. We had no indication of the location of the grave, but hoped we could find it fairly quickly. There was a ruined church, or chapel, on the Island, and my wife suggested that may be a good place to start.

As we neared the island, I was struck by the lack of suitable landing places. The island seemed quiet, peaceful, but strangely unwelcoming.

Finally, I saw a short flat beach area pebbled with black or dark grey pebbles, which seemed our best choice. But as we started our run in, the calm water broke into a number of ripples, and 4 heads appeared around the boat, causing initial consternation, until our companion called out they were seals. We made a safe landing. The island seemed deathly quiet. We briefly looked at the ruined churches and noted they were of great age. Thick lichen and moss covered them. We could not find any discernible graves. One of my companions asked what we should do next.

This is a question I had been considering, and as I looked back across the loch I tried to imagine the scene 300 years earlier, when the slain chief's sons had brought him here. Finally, I said we need to leave the church and climb that hill. When asked what made me think the grave was there, I replied;

"If I had come here to bury my father, that is the place I would choose, the highest point on the Island, overlooking the pass at Glencoe, the family's home."

Nothing further was said; we ascended the hill and saw a small memorial with two slate inserts, the first of which carried the inscription The Burial place of MacDonald of Glencoe. We now found ourselves standing in front of the grave we came to find. Here on that windswept hill, the old chief, who had put his trust in a Campbell, lay in peace. We took some photographs and said a quiet prayer for the souls of the MacDonalds of Glencoe.

While at Glencoe, we took a walk through the glen. The glen had obviously changed in the 300 years since the massacre. Back then there was no proper village, just a huddle of farms and crofts. Spread along the Burn (Creek) that meandered through the site, the actual landscape including the imposing mountain the Pap of Glencoe had likely changed little. However, there was an eerie atmosphere apparent to both me and my wife. It is difficult to put into words. Some years later I got a similar feeling when visiting the Alamo in San Antonio Texas Friends of mine, tell me of similar feelings when they visited The USS Arizona in Pearl Harbour and the Gettysburg battlefield in Pa.

I know not every visitor senses this, when standing at a location where so many people died and I cannot explain why.

A few days later we left Glencoe to continue our holiday, heading for Culloden Moor where some of my ancestors also lie in peace. But we left the Glen with a heavy heart. My wife had shed a tear at the site of the massacre, and I vowed I would one day tell their story. Cruel is the Snow is my tribute to the innocent victims of the most heinous crime that can be committed in Scotland, Murder under Trust. May they forever find peace in the arms of our Lord.

Laird Stephen C. Challis

Chapter 1

A New Dawn and a New King

Dawn broke over a cold London population. Thick smoke lay low over the streets as the frost covering the thatched roofs slowly dissipated. It could, in fact, be a day like any other February day in 17th Century England, but not quite. Today was February the 13th, in the year of our Lord 1689. After a tumultuous year of strife and uncertainty, England was about to get a new king and queen.

The couple barely knew each other, and it was certainly no love match. At 26 years, the bride was certainly of the Royal line; her grandfather was no lesser luminary than Charles Stuart, Charles the 1st of England who had been executed following the Civil war. Her father was King James, the Second, an unpopular monarch who had fled after Williams's arrival in England at the behest of the English Parliament, and who was now in exile in France. Mary had married William, 12 years her senior, not for love or any of the romantic ideals, but purely out of duty. Such was the way in European royal circles.

William had also been born to royal parents. His father was William, the Second of Orange, and King of the Netherlands. They had been married in 1677, when Mary had been just 14 years old. The arranged marriage had been put together in an attempt to restore relations between England and the Netherlands following a bitter war between the two nations. Neither was required to give their consent.

William had landed in England on the 5th of November, 1688, with a fleet of 463 ships, and at the head of 14,000 troops. It was not co-incidence that he chose this date. November the 5th was Guy Fawkes Day, a popular national holiday in England, following the discovery of a plot to assassinate King James, by blowing up Parliament with barrels of gunpowder placed under it in a cellar some 85 years earlier.

Previously a celebration of James' deliverance from the Catholic plotters, William now proclaimed the day should also be used to commemorate his liberation of the English people from the Catholics, with himself as the Liberator. He had proved a popular choice, and crowds had lined the route to London, swelling his army to over 2,000 men by the time he reached London. Mary, though apprehensive of the future, was nevertheless glad to be back in London, and she seemed a popular choice to the people.

However, beneath the surface, all was not as well in the kingdom. Although Parliament had passed the act of succession to allow William to become king, the decision was not unanimous, and William Sancroft, the Archbishop of Canterbury, whom tradition dictated should perform the ceremony, had refused to do so, believing that King James was still the rightful king. Parliament had then appointed Henry Compton, the Bishop of London, to perform the ceremony.

As the morning wore on, soldiers began to take up positions lining the route to Westminster Abbey, where the coronation would take place. At the appointed time, William and his wife emerged from their residence and took their place under the silk canopy held aloft on 8 poles; they walked sedately flanked by the royal guard. The crowds were already lining the streets, and the soldiers were having some difficulty in holding them back. If there were any detractors, they were invisible. Cheers and waves filled the streets and spring flowers paved their route. Mary smiled and waved a little apprehensively. Her husband had no such concerns, nodding occasionally, and waving regally at the crowd in acknowledgement. Away from the pomp and ceremony of London, however, things were far from joyous. In Ireland, support for the exiled King James was growing. North of the Border in Scotland, bitter resentment was taking root. England was anything but a tranquil nation.

While the coronation was taking place in the usual celebratory fashion; in London, 400 miles to the north, many Scots were far from happy at the news.

Mary's father, the former king, was intent on regaining his throne, and had rallied formidable opposition in Scotland to the declaration of William as king.

It was under this turbulent background, and following their coronation that William and Mary, now settled in the royal residence of Kensington palace, received a visitor some short few weeks after their coronation.

The Lord High Chancellor of England, John Somers was, arguably the most senior advisor to the monarch. A tall, measured diplomat, Somers knew the ways and means of the monarchy better than most. The royal Herald announced him, and he duly entered and bowed with an air of almost comical formality.

The chancellor carried with him a rolled letter, which he unfurled and read aloud.

"Your most gracious majesties I bring troublesome news from you most loyal subjects to the north of your kingdom. They concern the actions of the most despicable and outrageous rogues Sir Ewen Cameron of Lochiel, the clan chief of the Cameron family and those of his treacherous underdog Viscount of Dundee John Graham. Both have refused to swear allegiance to your majesties and Dundee now rides north to the highlands to raise an army against you."

He finished the letter and bowed, awaiting a response.

William smiled at his wife before replying.

"Good sir, we thank you for your consul in this matter. Now what to do?"

He tried to suppress the sarcasm, but his smile again to Mary gave his true thoughts away.

The Chancellor seemed a bit annoyed, especially as Mary tried to suppress a grin; however, unlike her husband, Mary, was not ready to dismiss the news so lightly.

"Tell us Lord Chancellor, and you may speak to us freely; what threat do these Highland rebels pose to our persons and our mighty realm?"

William was now smiling broadly at his young wife.

The Chancellor stood up, and without emotion, replied.

"None, sire, to your realm as individuals. They do not seek your throne, nor to rule in your stead."

William could not contain himself any longer and allowed a short laugh.

"Well then, it would be foolish and most un-kingly for us to think so, would it not?"

"I feel, my good lord Chancellor that your concern for our person is admirable, but we cannot concern ourselves with such tantrums. I am sure our loyal subjects of our beloved Scotland can take care of these rebels. Do you not think, my lord?"

The Chancellor believed nothing of the sort, but realised he had not made the matter clear. So did Mary, who interjected.

"Tell us truthfully, Lord Chancellor, is there something more we should know about these rebels, something that you have not told us?"

His queen had given the Lord Chancellor a lifeline, and he gratefully took it.

"Your Majesty's, my concern is not for the threat posed by these individuals, for they need be paid no heed. It is for the cause they support. They have no ambitions to seek the throne for themselves; rather, they seek to reinstate your father, James, in your place. In England and Scotland, there are many of these so called Jacobites. The real threat would come should they all unite."

Mary nodded, a gesture noted by the king. She knew that there were a number of people opposed to her and William, and among these were many of the Highland clans and clan chiefs; principle among them was John Graham, First Viscount of Dundee, a proud lowland Scot and Episcopalian. He planned with others who were loyal to King, to summon a convention at Sterling in King James's name. This group may prove to be the first genuine test of the new rulers in London.

William's smile had vanished, to be replaced with a steeled look of determination, as Somers words sank in. He quickly thanked the Lord Chancellor, who bowed and made a hasty exit, leaving the King and queen to digest the news.

William knew James was still a threat. He also knew that the lands of Scotland were a breeding ground for insurrection. Clearly, he must take action. The honeymoon was over. Immediately, he summoned his top military commander, General Mackay, to attend the palace.

In addition to being King, William was a career soldier and knew that the Scots posed no real threat to his reign on their own, but the possibility of a return of King James and his supporters, with Highland Clan backing, was a different matter. He turned to a trusted ally, General Hugh Mackay of Scourie. Mackay was a loyal Highlander who had been in Dutch service with the Scots Brigade for many years. He was a man whose loyalty to William, and the Dutch was unwavering. William had rewarded his loyalty by appointing him commander in Chief of the army in Scotland. He would, therefore, be the ideal choice to crush this rebellion.

Mackay eagerly accepted the challenge; this was his chance to prove his mettle to his Sovereign. He left the audience with the king, armed with a royal decree to pursue and destroy the rebels. Mackay lost no time in preparing, and in June he left for Scotland at the head of 3,400 men that were split into 3 regiments that included a substantial contingent of 500 mounted cavalry.

From a hill overlooking the renovated palace of Hampton Court, William watched his army depart, resplendent in their uniforms of red and gold. It was certainly an impressive sight. An enormous crowd had gathered to see them off. Wives and sweethearts shouted encouragement. The King's army was going to war, and the sight was nothing short of magnificent. The King had contemplated accompanying them, but more news had come from France that was unsettling. James was not only sowing insurrection in Scotland but also in France. The French had a navy and should they side with James, they could mount an invasion across the channel, which would pose a genuine threat. For his part, James was indeed planning to retake his throne but, his force was still inferior to Williams. His attention turned to Ireland, where a sizable group of his supporters was ready to join him. William, for his part, bided his time and waited while he obtained extra intelligence from his agents in France. Meanwhile, the English Army headed for the border with Scotland, and to their destiny at a place called Killiecrankie.

Chapter 2

The Charismatic Bonnie Dundee

Bonnie Dundee *by Sir Walter Scott*[1]

To the Lords of Convention 'twas Claver'se who spoke,
"Ere the King's crown shall fall, there are crowns to be broke;
So let each Cavalier who loves honour and me,
Come follow the bonnet of Bonny Dundee.
Chorus:
Come fill up my cup, come fill up my can,
Come saddle your horses, and call up your men;
Come open the West Port and let me gang free,
And it's room for the bonnets of Bonny Dundee!'
Dundee he is mounted, he rides up the street,
The bells are rung backward, the drums they are beat;
But the Provost, douce man, said, "Just e'en let him be,
The Gude Town is weel quit of that Deil of Dundee.'
"Away to the hills, to the caves, to the rocks—
Ere I own a usurper, I'll couch with the fox—
And tremble, false Whigs, in the midst of your glee,
You have not seen the last of my bonnet and me!'
He waved his proud hand, and the trumpets were blown,
The kettle-drums clashed, and the horsemen rode on,
Till on Ravelston's cliffs, and on Clermiston's lee,
Died away the wild war-notes of Bonny Dundee.
Chorus:
Come fill up my cup, come fill up my can.
Come saddle the horses and call up the men,
Come open your gates, and let me gae free,
For it's up with the bonnets of Bonny Dundee.

---

1. *https://www.poetrynook.com/poet/sir-walter-scott*

Four hundred (400) miles to the north, Highland nobleman John Graham of Claverhouse, better known to history as Viscount Dundee, or more affectionately as Bonnie Dundee, was enjoying the hospitality of Edinburgh castle. The charismatic highland chief had just successfully called a convention of the clans opposed to William and Mary's reign, and had gathered a number of clans to his cause, to rally to the good king James banner. He now had a formidable army of the most belligerent highland clans, ready to take on the Williamites, as the highlanders dubbed William's men. The mood in Edinburgh was celebratory.

However, Dundee was an experienced commander and knew that he would need to fight the King's Army eventually. Jacobite spies had been dispatched to London to gauge the new kings' response. Meanwhile, he basked in the adulation of the highland clans.

However, all this political rhetoric was not universally infecting Scotland. One hundred and twenty miles to the North West, in the highlands near Fort William, 19 year old Annella MacDonald was catching her breath after a stiff climb up the small mountain known as The Pap of Glencoe. The structure was just under two and a half thousand feet high, and gave commanding views over the picturesque Loch Leven.

Annella often came here, when she needed to reflect and consider some decision or another but she had not climbed it for some months, not since her man, Donald McBane, a soldier in The Earl of Mars Regiment of Foot, based near inverness, had visited her. The cap of shale slate at the peak was popular for courting couples. She had happy memories of Donald sharing this special place with her. She had not seen him for almost six months, not since the winter snows had swept the glen in 1688. Now, with the onset of spring, her thoughts returned to Donald and the time they had first met, here at the summit two years ago. The highlands were peaceful then. Donald was a tobacco spinner apprentice and had shown no real interest in political matters, but they had often discussed the situation in England, and the rise of William of Orange, King of the Netherlands, who had married into the English Royal family. Annella had no real interest in such matters, and usually tried to turn the conversation back to more important subjects, such as trying to bridge the gap between Donald and her father, who was unsure of the young Scot, who had apparently captured his daughters' heart, but that was over a year ago.

Donald had become friendly with the redcoats at Ballachulish and, in particular, Captain Kenneth McKenzie, who had seen potential in the young Scot and given him some lessons in sword fighting that usually ended with him being disarmed within a few minutes. Finally, Donald had decided to make a move. As she sat on the peak, her mind went back to their last meeting, the walk through the glen alongside the burn.

"I just don't see why you needed to be a soldier; it's not as if there is a war on Donald. There's a good life here in the highlands, and you had a good trade."

Donald looked away across the heather strewn landscape before replying.

"Spinning Tobacco for old men to smoke themselves into their graves, you mean?"

He turned back to face her and placed his hands gently on her shoulders.

"You're a bonnie girl, Annella, but I cannot see myself spending all my life in the tobacco trade. Captain Robert says I have the making of a fine soldier in the King's army. He said I could get a commission and become an officer. An officer is a man of substance and the pay is good." he paused. *"Good enough to support a wife."*

She looked up at him and said nothing for a moment, then smiled, the sort of coy smile that she knew he had difficulty in resisting.

"Why Donald McBane, are you making me an offer?"

Donald faltered and fumbled his reply.

"Oh n-no, well not, n-not offer but, w-well, a man needs to think of such things, l-like in the future."

Annella laughed.

"The future, oh I see, so in the future, when you have become an officer and have a position, then you may come back to Glencoe again and ask for my hand."

Donald paused and answered carefully, falling immediately into the deep hole she had dug for him.

"W-well, yes, that would be right and proper, would it not?"

Annella slammed the proverbial door.

"And how do you think my husband and bairns would feel about that?"

Donald looked confused.

"Husband? What bairns? You're not married."

Annella moved in close and kissed him lightly on the cheek.

"Who knows what the future hold for any of us? You are going for to be a soldier, and me; the good lord may have other plans for me."

Back on the Pap, Annella smiled softly to herself at the memory. She had not heard from Donald for almost 6 months. But talk around the table was of growing political troubles in the south. The nation had a new king, in fact two kings, who were squaring up for a war. The English parliament had backed King William, who had wed Mary, the sister of James, who many - including her father - saw as the rightful heir. According to her father, even now, an English Army was marching north towards her beloved highlands.

But here, overlooking the peaceful, mist covered Loch Leven; such matters seemed distant, remote from the turmoil in the south. She stood up and began the journey back down the mountain.

Little could Annella have known that at that very time, the subject of her thoughts was marching with McKay's army towards the Scottish border.

The Clan chiefs gathered at Edinburgh were not too concerned. 400 years earlier, another English army had taken on the Scots and was decimated by the highlanders under William Wallace. The spirt of Wallace still ran deep through the highlands. So Dundee was confident.

Word soon reached him of the approaching English Army. He had respect for McKay, but knew his tactics were unsuited to the highlands. Now, at a strategy meeting of clan chiefs, he laid out his plan. Stretching a large map of Scotland on the oak table in the main dining hall, he addressed the assembled clan chiefs.

"McKay's army will look for good ground to fight. He has the numbers to beat us in a one to one standoff. The last sighting we had was here."

Dundee pointed to a point on the map close to the Scots border.

"We would expect him to gather the army at Sterling and rest before marching north."

"At his present progress, we can expect him in 4 or 5 days. Now, he will need to enter the highlands through the pass at Killiecrankie. He is no fool and will be expecting us to confront him as he enters. We'll no oblige him though. Let his advance units pass through with nae bother. When his lead section gets through, then we hit him head on. He will be blocked in the pass, then we'll show him the highland charge."

"The Williamites have one weakness: they canna use their muskets and the bayonet together. And I've never met a lowlander yet who can match the Highland Claymore."

The clan chiefs broke into laughter.

Dawn broke on the 27th of July at Killiecrankie pass. As the mist slowly dispersed, Dundee observed the approaching redcoat army, their banners flowing in the light breeze. He could just make out the section of mounted cavalry together with several mounted riders he took to be officers. Dundee had reached the pass the day before and had taken up position overlooking the valley. His army of 2,500 men was no real match for the 4,600 redcoat infantry and the accompanying 500 mounted cavalry in a straightforward battle.

But Dundee had no intention of giving McKay a standard battle. All morning and into the afternoon, the English trudged forward. By 4pm, the lead elements of the English army reached the pass and slowed. McKay sensed danger and scanned the craggy outcrops for the enemy with his spyglass. There were no visible signs of activity, and after an hour, McKay ordered a troop of cavalry forward.

They returned after reporting the pass seemed clear. Dundee was impressed by the size of McKay's forces. He gave strict instructions for his Highlanders to hold position and keep down. The highlanders waited, expecting McKay to enter the pass and charge. However, they were disappointed. Dundee now pulled a master stroke, sending his 50 strong cavalry unit into the pass and into direct sight of the enemy. McKay took the bait, and assuming the cavalry units were a skirmish line, formed column and advanced three ranks deep, moving rapidly forward and sending the highlanders into full retreat. Or so it seemed. The General smiled to himself. These Highland rebels had little stomach for a fight. He would pursue them until they turned to face him, then he would move the entire army against them in one last charge.

With over half the English column now deep into the pass, McKay realised he had ridden into a trap. Rounding the bluff, he caught sight of the main Jacobite force occupying the high bluff on each side of the pass. He knew that a frontal attack would draw heavy fire from the high ground. Instead, McKay opened fire with three cannon, his entire artillery component. The cannon fire had little effect, the gunners being unable to gain sufficient elevation to hit the clansmen above them. The balls smashing into the granite bluff a good 20 feet below them. This brought forth a bellow of laughter from Dundee's men/ in response, Dundee sent 20 marksmen from his Cameron's detachment forward, to fire on the exposed redcoat lines. Being better marksmen, the snipers took their toll on McKay's raw men, forcing them to pull back. However, Dundee knew that the setting sun was directly in front of the highland front line, blinding them and giving the redcoats an advantage. Patiently, he waited for it to drop below the mountain top. McKay was confused. Mistaking the hesitancy for fear, he ordered his infantry forward to lay down fire on the pass sides.

Dundee watched as the English musket men took up position and open fire. At such extreme range, there was little effect. Using the natural rock cover, the highlanders now moved down through the rocky sides of the pass. The sun was no longer a factor. The firing grew more sporadic. Most of the redcoats surmised that the highlanders were waiting for nightfall to affect a retreat and avoid casualties. It was a grievous error.

At less than 200 yards, the order was given, and over two thousand highlanders wielding claymores, axes, and muskets rose up and charged into the front, and both flanks of McKay's army. The three pronged attack highland charge smashed into the English flanks, quickly breaking the Loyalists line, and they fell back.in disarray Two or 3 volleys of fire were loosed off, but with minimal effect. On the left flank, from his vantage point, Dundee watched as the king's army began throwing small orbs that trailed smoke. These were mystifying to the clansmen, until they exploded on striking the ground, sending shards of metal and rock into their ranks. The early grenades had little effect, however, and some were dropped prematurely when the grenadiers throwing them were hit, and dropped them in the loyalist ranks.

The panicking Redcoats managed a last volley that cut through the Highlanders ranks, killing around 800 men before they stopped and sent a return volley of fire into the redcoats, who were frantically trying to reload. Discarding their muskets, the Highlanders crashed into the panic-stricken redcoats, slashing and hacking with swords, axes, and hammers. For a while, the Hastings Regiment, under the command of

Colonel Fernando Hastings, held their ground, but Dundee's Jacobite cavalry charged into them, finally putting them to flight. The bulwark of McKay's army was mainly filled with lowlanders, who had already developed a healthy respect for the wild highlander clans. Now, in sheer panic, many threw down their empty muskets and ran. Others quickly fitted the guns with the plug bayonet, turning the gun into a useful spear, but also making it un-fireable. Many redcoats were struck by spinning axes thrown by the clansmen. Many more were decapitated by the mighty two handed claymores. The screams of the wounded and dying now filled the evening air, mingling with the screams of the wounded and dying, along with the blood curdling battle cry of the Highland Army, who now sensed blood. The rampaging highlanders cut through the redcoat ranks with the efficiency of a swarm of locust. Hundreds fell, screaming and begging for mercy. Dismembered bodies lay everywhere.

McKay was aware of the danger to his whole army, and he ordered his entire cavalry forward to counter the attack. Drawing his sword, he led the charge himself, urging the infantry to fall in behind. In return, Dundee sent his smaller cavalry force to support the highland charge. Despite the lead shown by their commander, the redcoat infantry did not follow McKay. Sensing a quick victory, the highlanders closed around the commander of the English force. Somewhat miraculously, McKay survived the assault; hacking and slashing his way clear to reach high ground with the survivors of his cavalry. From there, he witnessed in horror the destruction of his entire force.

However, the Battle did not all go the Scots' way.

Amid the white smoke and carnage, sat slumped against a standing rock, was the mortally wounded commander of the highlanders, Viscount Dundee, a jagged wound from a musket ball oozing blood onto his tunic. He watched with fading eyesight as the redcoat army was put to full flight, streaming back out of the pass. The victor of Killiecrankie would not survive the battle, but his name and deeds still reverberate through Scottish folklore to this day, when patriots recall the valour of Bonnie Dundee.

Donald McBane was one of the redcoats facing Dundee's highlanders that day. Having fired during the last volley, he now sprinted back down the pass, and to his horror, saw the highlanders move to cut off his retreat. Desperately, he moved through the heather, pursued by a highlander wielding a broadsword, who fired his pistol at him. The shot missed, the ball passing two feet high and to the left. He continued to dodge and weaved for a while, out manoeuvring his pursuer until he reached a promontory looking out across the babbling cataract and kirk, and to safety beyond.

McBane looked at the gap; it must have been at least 20 feet. He turned back just as three clansmen emerged from the bushes only yards from him. One lowered his axe and drew his basket hilt. The clansmen were highlanders from the Clan the MacDonalds of Glencoe, the same clan that Annella belonged to. Donald could not have known that this particular clan would be in the battle. He only knew that for now he faced the determined clansman armed with just his empty rifle and plug bayonet. His opponent raised his shield and moved determinedly forward.

"Yea na where to run, Laddie," he grunted as he moved in for the kill.

Donald did not reply. He moved deftly and purposely towards the clansman, who could not believe he was intending to fight them all, and they were right. Without warning, he dropped his musket and swept his hat from his head before he turned and ran full speed for the bluff. He launched himself out over the kirk, to the astonishment of the clansmen. Incredibly, he cleared the kirk, but crashed into the far bank, severely bruising his arms and shins, and losing a shoe into the foaming water below. However, he scrambled up the escarpment with assistance from other survivors above him. On the far bank, the clansman surprise, turned into a cheer. As McBane looked back, he was sure he heard a shout from the MacDonald on the other side.

"Next time Laddie."

The survivors pulled back from the pass. The Highlanders had won the day, but at great cost. Their charismatic commander was dead, and the Jacobites knew that the Royalists would be back.

As McKay reached the safety of Stirling castle, 61 miles south of the battle, he was aware of the enormity of the defeat. Of the five thousand troops he had entered the pass with; a mere 500 were left alive. News of the battle reached Glencoe a few days later, and toasts were drunk to brave Bonnie Dundee. Annella was not as happy, however. She knew that the defeat would not go unchallenged. War was coming to the highlands, and it seemed increasing likely that she and Donald would be on opposite sides.

The gap that McBane cleared was later measured at 18 feet. The spot has been known ever since as 'The Soldiers Leap' and has become one of Scotland's biggest tourist attractions.

Chapter 3

Dundalk

The victory at Killiecrankie was, of course, marred by Dundee's death. He was buried at Blair House, and the Jacobite army now fell under the command of Colonel Alexander Cannon. His plans for a follow up attack stalled, when 60-year-old Clan Chief, Sir Ewen Cameron of Lochiel, one of the most formidable Highland chiefs, was side-lined when the council appointed Cannon to command over him. Cameron was so insulted; he had promptly left, taking some of his clan with him. This depleted the highland army, but nonetheless, Cannon felt he could easily defeat the King's garrison at the town of Dunkeld.

While the Jacobite's prepared to march on the town, the loyalist commander of the Cameroonian Regiment, Lieutenant Colonel William Cleland, was studying a letter he had received from the Scottish Privy Council, ordering him to move from his base in Perth to the city of Dunkeld, and to hold it against all odds.

Cleland was none too pleased. He knew Dunkeld was without any walls or fortifications. He was also acutely aware of the size of his force of twelve hundred men, compared to that of Cannons' five thousand highlanders. Clearly, the advantage was with Cannon. Clearly, the smart move would be to pull back to Perth and regroup, but to disregard the order would have, in effect, been disregarding the King. Reluctantly, he gave orders for the regiment to move out.

Upon arrival at the town, a quick inspection of its fortifications confirmed his fears. Realising that he had little chance to successfully engage the army outside the town, Cleland therefore ordered his men to fall back onto the cathedral and its high surrounding wall. For the next two days, remnants of the King's army also reached the town and were quickly integrated into the defence. Among them was the young Donald McBane, battered and bruised, but with an incredible tale to tell. He was also now the proud possessor of a basket hilt sword, picked up from a dead highlander. The sword had a strip of tartan on its grip, a strip of MacDonald tartan.

However, the bulk of McKay's army had retreated to Perth to regroup. Cleland could expect no help from that quarter. He was on his own.

Quickly, the defenders occupied the Cathedral and fortified the surrounded stoutly built houses. They did not have long to wait. Cannon's scouts reported that the loyalist army was now in the town, occupying the fortified cathedral and its high walls. The residents wisely either evacuated or locked themselves in their homes. Cannon, realising that slaughtering townspeople would hardly endear him to the Scots, ordered the Highlanders to go straight for the jugular.

The Jacobites surged into the town and threw themselves at the cathedral wall. Well aimed fire from the ramparts stalled the attack, and the highlanders, unable to employ the Highland charge, that had served them so well at Killiecrankie, due to the narrow streets; instead turned on the fortified houses outside, and when unable to break in, they torched them, burning many of the occupants alive.

Rallying his beleaguered troops, Colonel Cleland was struck by two musket balls; one punctured his side, embedding itself into his liver, the other struck him in the head. The commander fell mortally wounded, but managed to drag himself out of sight, assisted by some close aides. His dying words were to keep his death from the men, lest they lose heart.

For six hours the battle raged, until running out of ammunition, the Highlanders retreated, leaving three hundred of their dead behind. It was a hollow victory. Redcoat bodies littered the ground, and the royalists were also critically short of ammunition.

For the Highlanders, the failure to take the Cathedral was a bitter blow, and they laid the blame squarely on their Commanders' shoulders. The army marched away, and the chiefs let the Privy Council know, in no uncertain terms, that they would not return until a new commander, of the calibre of Dundee, was forthcoming. The English had stopped the Jacobite rebellion in its tracks, at least for now.

The highland army now paused to take stock, and an emissary was sent to King James requesting reinforcements.

24

Chapter 4

Call for Help

In London, the news of the success at Dunkeld in Scotland was received well by the people, but the King had little time to celebrate. In March, James had returned to Ireland, landing on the 12th of March at Kinsale in County Cork, from which he marched on Dublin, where he was now located, and from where he was consolidating his army of Dutch and Irish patriots. Confident the MacKay's army could take care of the Scots problem, the King appointed veteran soldier, Fredrick Schomberg, the 1st Duke of Schomberg, as commander of his forces in Ireland, and dispatched him to Bangor Bay in Ulster at the head of 20,000 troops. At first, things had gone well; but now, not so much, after capturing the town of Carrick Fergus with little resistance, but had shown little stomach to move on James. Dispatches from Schomberg's camp had revealed that he had around 6,000 troops less than James, and many of them were poorly armed with old style matchlocks or just small farm implements, such as pitchforks.

****

The highland army now paused to take stock, the highlanders dispersed back to their homes, and the Privy Council appointed aging Clan Chief, Sir Ewan Cameron, a man of 60, who had fought under Dundee at Killiecrankie, to command the remnants of the scattered highland army. It was of course, only a stopgap measure. The council quickly decided the best course of action was to send an emissary to King James, requesting reinforcements for the Scottish Jacobites.

****

The Imposing Chateau of St Germain-en-Laye in France lies 19 kilometres west of the city of Paris. This Royal residence had been placed at the disposal of King James by French monarch, Louis XIV, and it was here that the emissaries from the Privy Council were received by James and his aides.

The King's appearance came as a shock to the highlanders. He seemed pale, underweight, and seemed to be unsure of his words at times.

However, after several meetings, the King gave his answer. The pending campaign in Ireland would prevent him from sending troops, this was in part due to the fact, that a large part of James' army was French and Irish, and the French were less inclined to support the Highlanders, whose local support was patchy to say the least. In Ireland, the bulk of the population was protestant and far more amenable to James. This came as a bitter blow to the emissaries. However, the King stated he would supply equipment, weapons, and ammunition, plus one of his most trusted commanders, Major General, Thomas Buchan, and some more junior officers. The Emissaries gratefully accepted the offer before taking a ship back to Scotland.

William was not used to these delays, nor did he see any reason to continue to give James time to consolidate his position. Today, he had gathered his advisors at Windsor to debate the situation. Emissaries from MacKay's army had reported that the Jacobite army in Scotland had scattered after Dunkeld. Therefore, the situation in Scotland was contained. It was time to confront James' head on. With him defeated, killed, or captured, the Scottish problem would evaporate. The King spoke;

"We pay no heed to the rebellious scots tribes. For they are leaderless now, with the traitor Dundee dead in his grave. The English army will cross to Ireland and put an end to this insurrection."

"I feel we can put our trust in General McKay to bring these rebellious highlanders to heel." He proclaimed.

"The situation in our beloved Ireland is, however, different. We will raise a second army to support General Schomberg. I will command this force. And we will surely vanquish the forces of James once and forever."

The King's words brought a chorus of agreement from the court.

27

....

Chapter 5

Buchan's Defeat

In Early March 1690, Buchan arrived at the Highland town of Keppoch with his officers to meet the assembled clan chiefs, and plan the next steps in the campaign. Agreement was far from unified; some clans felt that a wiser course would be to submit to Williams' rule and negotiate with the English. However, the older and wiser chiefs knew that previous trust of the English had proved to be badly misguided. Buchan spoke confidently of the certainty of King James prevailing against William's army in the impending clash in Ireland. He also pointed out that William's second army, raised by him to support Schomberg in Ireland, had left the English unable to mount a campaign against the Scots. In short, now was the time to strike.

The argument won the day, however, action was deferred for a few weeks, to allow scots farmers to attend to the spring planting season.

In the interim, the council decided to place a contingent of 1,200 highland infantry under Buchan's command and instructed him to secure the lowlands borders and keep the enemy from moving north. Had Buchan complied, the course of history may well have been changed. However, ignoring advice from the clan chiefs not to advance south past Culnakill, he continued the march along the river Spey, towards the town of Cromdale, in Inverness-shire. Due to desertion and disillusionment among his force, Buchan's force had dwindled to 800 men. He camped on the bank of the Spey on 30th April. Inexplicably for a man of such military experience, Buchan did not send out scouts or post sentries overnight, convinced the English were falling back.

By dawn the following day, a larger force of redcoats under Sir Thomas Livingston, of the Inverness Garrison had gathered on the bank opposite them. Lack of scouts from the Scots had meant that the force was not detected until they began crossing the river. The alarm was raised, but it was all too late. Half of the sleeping highlanders had no time to reach their weapons before Livingstone had dispatched 6 troops of mounted dragoon cavalry into their midst, in advance of his spearhead of 800 Grants, supported by 3 regiments of foot. The cavalry rode through the Highland camp slashing and trampling the panic stricken clansmen. The result was carnage. A small band of determined highlanders made a brief stand on the bank, but were quickly wiped out. It seemed that the entire highland army was about to be wiped from the face of the earth.

But providence intervened when a thick rolling mist descended from the mountains, enveloping the battlefield and forcing Livingstone to call off the attack. By the time the fog cleared, over 400 highlanders were dead or captured; more were hunted down and separated into small groups.

The opposition to William's rule was effectively over. MacKay sent a messenger to the King informing him of the victory.

Chapter 6

The Battle of the Boyne

Meanwhile, in Ireland, the situation remained fairly stagnant. Schomberg and his 36,000 troops, and James with his 23,000, faced off against each other and waited. James's army comprised mainly peasants and Irish cavalry, recruited from among the Irish gentry; however, it also included 6,000 French troops. The numeric advantage should have spurred Schomberg to launch an immediate attack, however, he had stalled. And King William had lost patience. On June 14th, 1690, he sailed into Carrickfergus in Ulster, at the head of 16,000 fresh troops. The intent was to take Dublin and scatter the Jacobite army once and for all. William reached Dundalk where the bulk of Schomberg's army was encamped, and the two armies merged, creating a total force of 36,000 loyalist troops.

Between William and the city was the river Boyne, a deep flowing river that afforded few crossing points. One of these lay close to the village of Drogheda, where the river spread out over a pebble bottom, affording a good fording point for men and horses. James knew he had to defend the city, and meeting William on open ground invited disaster. James knew his only chance was to hold William at the Boyne. He moved his army to cover the Ford.

James's deputy was an Irish nobleman, Richard Talbot, who held the title First Earl of Tyrconnell, and Lord Deputy of Ireland. On the morning of June 28th, he was summoned to the King's marquee. The King had cast the die and now wanted to hear Talbots' view of their chances.

Talbot moved to a map set on a table in the marquee and scanned it momentarily.

"Well sire, the enemy has superior numbers, that's a fact sure enough, but they will have to cross the river here."

He indicated a point on the map.

"That means they will be bunched up pretty tight. They will try to secure a foothold on our side, and this will enable them to bring more troops across. You will need to place our best troops at the crossing point to block the advance."

The King nodded.

"Agreed, my Lord Earl. That would be O'Neill's Dragoons. If they can halt the advance, then we can engage them with supporting musket fire from the bank. But William will know this, and I would expect him to use his regiment of Blue Guards to lead the attack. They are highly disciplined Dutch troops and possibly the finest in his army."

King James knew this, and also that the odds were not in his favour.

"What about the men, my Lord Earl? Will they fight?"

Talbot hesitated before replying. He had to choose his words carefully. He had reviewed the Jacobite forces and noted most were not professional soldiers, rather; they were peasants and farmers, keen but poorly trained. Less than half had firearms, and those that did, had the obsolete firelock (matchlock), a smooth-bore musket that was none too accurate over 50 yards. In addition, those without firelocks were armed with a mixture of farm and smithy tools, including Scythes, sickles, axes and hammers. There were some swords, but few were trained in their use. The Jacobite did have an efficient cavalry unit which was well trained, and probably the best troops in James's army. He could hardly tell James what he really thought.

"Well, sire, the men are fiercely loyal to you. They have little love for the Catholic cause, or the Dutch puppet king. They are itching for a fight, so they are. William won't know what hit him when we turn them loose."

On the morning of July11th, William and his army reached the Boyne River, and for the first time saw the Jacobite forces, now arrayed before him, they were hardly an inspiring sight. One of his aides addressed the king.

"I think we will have an easy victory, sire. This petite bunch of peasants will scatter like leaves when the fighting starts."

William was not so sure.

"The land is none too even; the hills and dips in the land could hide several thousand more. I think we will test the mettle of these Jacobites. Bring the Blue Guard forward and let us see what cannon they have."

The Jacobite artillery opened fire as the Blue Guard advanced. William's canon responded. His were more numerous and the river valley soon filled with white smoke. Overall, the barrage was ineffectual. Some of William's cannon overshot the Jacobite lines and straddled the Village of Old Bridge on the far bank, damaging some of the houses. The advancing Dutch Blue Guard regiments now came within range of the enemy cannon. They were exposed and took some casualties, but held their line. Knowing that his officers would judge him as a commander under fire, William mounted his horse and called out to his aides.

"Good Sirs, I cannot see much from here. We will advance and observe from the bank."

The aides looked worried, and were debating whether this was a wise move, but had little choice but to agree; however, the decision was taken out of his hands when a battery of cannon opened fire from a concealed position in the hedges in front of the village. Their target was William's party. The gunners had been waiting for a suitable target, and when seeing William's banner, took their shot.

The lead shot and balls swept through the party. Several of William's escorts were hit, and the King himself was also grazed by a solid ball across the right shoulder.

He reeled and rocked in the saddle, but stayed mounted. Officers rushed to his aid. William was bruised but still very much in command; however, he abandoned the idea of a scouting mission.

That evening, William called his generals to a council of war. Schomberg put forward a plan to assault the Jacobite lines. It was a sound plan and William's English officers agreed it would serve them best by splitting James' forces and weakening them. However, the commander of the Blue Guard felt that they should lead a full frontal assault on the centre of the Jacobite line. To do less would expose them to a charge of cowardice in front of this peasant rabble army.

William considered both plans, but decided on his own.

"I will move with my main force here."

He indicated a small village named Slains, approximately 5 miles to the west.

"This will be a ruse to draw James's forces from the centre to protect his flank. We will then switch the attack to Old Bridge while James is dividing his force."

He then turned to Schomberg.

"Your son Meinhardt will commence a turning movement at the ford at Rosnaree, and push the enemy back, leaving them no choice but to retreat or get pushed into the river."

It was a sound plan. While his son attacked James's flank, Schomberg would lead the main assault at Old Bridge, supported by the Dutch Blue Guard.

He knew it would be a plan that his son would readily agree to.

Just after dawn on July 12, Meinhardt Schomberg, 3rd Duke of Schomberg, at the head of 3,000 troops, moved out of Williams's camp heading for Slane. This move came as a surprise to the Jacobite commanders. James had left that ford largely unprotected, save for a regiment of Dragoons under Sir Neil O'Neil. As he saw the superior force advancing, O'Neil ordered the Dragoons to dismount and take up firing positions. When the advance guard of Meinhardt's Grenadiers closed to less than one hundred yards, he gave the order to fire. Musket fire raked the advancing troops, and the line faltered, then closed ranks, and continued leaving dozens of dead in their wake. The Battle of the Boyne had begun.

Several more volleys cut into the Grenadiers and the advance halted. Through his spyglass, William saw this, and fearing they may turn back, ordered 4,000 English troops to break off and support Meinhardt's force. With sheer numbers, O'Neil's men faced annihilation. They fell back, taking horrendous casualties, including their commander, who was mortally wounded during the retreat.

James now faced the main frontal assault, but did not know from where. He was taken unawares by the situation at Rosnaree and mistakenly thought the main attack was coming from his flank, just as William had hoped. He hurriedly dispatched three quarters of his available men and 6 cannons to reinforce O'Neil's position. The battle at Rosnaree now developed into a furious standoff.

James's deployment had left the crossings at Old Bridge gravely weakened, to a garrison of 7,500 men. William now saw his chance and ordered the Blue Guard to advance. They did so, 1,900 strong and 10 ranks deep. They reached the river bank in perfect formation and strode straight in, holding their muskets above their heads to keep them protected from the fast flowing current. At the far bank, they briefly halted, levelled their muskets, took aim, and fired a devastating volley that tore into the Jacobite defenders. The Dutch were elite well-trained soldiers and were armed with the more reliable Snaphance muskets, a far superior weapon to the matchlock. They made no attempt to reload, but fixed socket bayonets and charged the line. The Defenders fell back into the ruins of Old Bridge and fierce hand to hand fighting broke out. Seeing the situation, the commander of the Irish Cavalry, until then, held in reserve; ordered his units forward under the command of James Fitz James, the 1st Duke of Berwick, who was also James's illegitimate son. The Blue Guards had all but cleared the Jacobite infantry from the town when Berwick's cavalry rode into them.

From a hill overlooking the battle, King William watched the drama unfold.

"Oh! My poor guards, my poor guards." William Exclaimed.

However, the Dutch were unphased by the attack, swiftly forming themselves into infantry squares and began firing into the mounted Jacobites. The battlefield became choked with shattered bodies of men and horses. Despite mounting losses, Berwick continued to mount charge after charge. Now, more and more regiments from Williams's army crossed the ford, expanding the beachhead and reinforcing the hard pressed guards. Among them, regiments of Huguenot and English infantry. In desperation, the Jacobites rushed to reinforce the line at the town entrance. They were mostly armed with farm implements and other tools. They did not, however, lack courage. The Infantry regiments lined up and delivered a catastrophic volley of musket fire that literally blew the Jacobite line apart. The survivors fell back in disarray.

Meanwhile, General Schomberg had led a fresh wave of infantry across the Boyne. He had nearly reached the bank, when a spirited attack by units of Berwick's cavalry reached him. In the ensuing hand fighting, the old Duke received several sabre cuts and was thrown from his horse. A cavalryman, realising he was a senior commander, fired his horse pistol at point blank range into the back of Schomberg's head. Other units from his command reached him and got him ashore, but he was mortally wounded and died within a few minutes.

The battle was slowly turning in William's favour. The Jacobite cavalry were pressing the attack with repeated charges, pushing the forces of William back towards the river. However, without the support of the infantry, regiments were now being decimated by the growing reinforcements streaming over the fords. The brave horsemen were taking massive casualties. The Blue Guard squares held and continued to pour accurate fire into the cavalry ranks. Berwick lost over a third of his force.

William now saw his chance. He mounted his horse, and while still keeping his right arm in a sling, led his Danish mercenaries forward. The tidal river was now rising. There were so many of them fording the river at the same time that it was acting like a damn, thus raising the water level forcing the Danes held their muskets over their heads as they waded across the water. As they emerged from the water's edge, they dropped into firing positions. Volley after volley cut into the collapsing Jacobite lines.

Now William could sense victory. He ordered his cavalry units, commanded by Baron Godert de Ginkel, to charge and sweep the remains of Berwick's horsemen from the field. William was now on the front line. His horse began to falter as it got caught in the oozing mud that was churned up by the mass troop crossing. In the confusion, a Dane fired at him, the ball whistling past his head. William tuned angrily at the offending soldier.

"Do you not know your own friends?"

De Ginkel men rode into the Jacobites, but despite their losses, Berwick responded to the challenge. William had intended to encircle the embittered Jacobite army and cut off any chance of retreat. But for that, he needed De Ginkel's force to break through Berwick's force. They failed. The two cavalry units clashed and fought sabre to sabre.

The Jacobites now began to fall back. Some mounted dragoons dismounted and took up defensive positions in the towns ruins. All in all, the rear guard held, slowing the Danish and Blue Guards' assault, and enabling most of the embattled Jacobites to flee the town.

Five miles away, a messenger reached James with news of the defeat at Old Bridge.

James was keen on pressing the attack home against Meinhardt, who had held his forces at bay all day. However, his French officers advised him to withdraw to a more defendable position. James reluctantly agreed. However, as the army fell back towards Duleek Bridge, they came across the routed forces from Old Bridge. The French tried to cross the Bridge against the flow, but were held by the sheer volume of men. Berwick's exhausted Jacobite Cavalry finally reached the Bridge, and finding it blocked both by fleeing infantry and fresh French troops themselves, finally broke. They forced their way through, scattering and trampling their own troops in an effort to evade the pursuing Blue Guard.

The situation had become grave; and James knew that if he could not stop the rout of his army, it faced total destruction. Watching the debacle from a nearby high point was Colonel Zurlauben. His French regiment had so far not seen action, and now he sized up the situation with military precision. He ordered the regiment to take position and fire a warning volley over the heads of the fleeing Jacobites. It worked with the headlong rush now stopped; the French took up position to cover the retreat, pouring volley after volley into Williams's men, forcing them back.

The army retreated to the city of Dublin, where the French urged James to take a ship to France while they remained to regroup. The defeated James reluctantly agreed.

Meanwhile, the cost of the Battle was being calculated. The Jacobites had lost around 1,500 men while Williams lost between 500 and 1,000. Not great by the standards of the day. The untrained and conscripts on both sides bore the bulk of the casualties. This was not a battle won by accurate weapons, good tactics, or the bravery of the participants. William had more men and used them to greater effect. In Ireland the struggle continued, the sword taken up by patriots like Patrick Sarsfield, who rose to fame as a fierce Irish Patriot. Sarsfield continued the campaign for 18 months. For William, Baron Ginkel continued to clash with the Jacobite's, but in effect, James' quest to retake the Throne of England was over.

Back in Scotland, news of James's defeat was not well received. There was now little hope of James being able to help the cause against William.

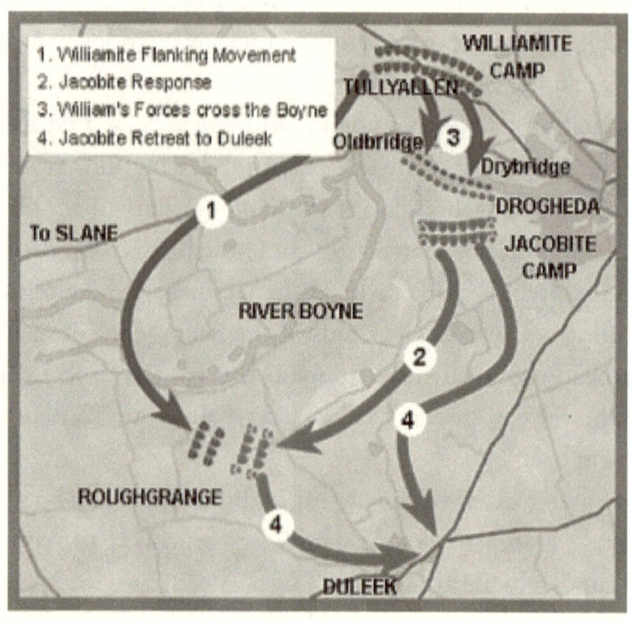
1. Williamite Flanking Movement
2. Jacobite Response
3. William's Forces cross the Boyne
4. Jacobite Retreat to Duleek
WILLIAMITE CAMP
TULLYALLEN
Oldbridge
Drybridge
DROGHEDA
JACOBITE CAMP
To SLANE
RIVER BOYNE
ROUGHGRANGE
DULEEK

Chapter 7

Strained Reunion

Following the defeat of James Army and the apparent collapse of opposition in Scotland, King William returned to London, an uneasy calm settled over the highlands. Though no outward signs of aggression were apparent, it was obvious that the spirit of defiance was still alive and well in the highlands.

The Clan Macdonald was spread across the Highlands in several branches. The Maclains of Glencoe were a smaller branch of the more numerous Macdonald's of Lochaber, both branches had a long history of cattle stealing and raiding. In the years leading up to Killiecrankie, the most frequent target of the belligerent clan, were the lands of Glenlyon and their owner, the Laird Robert Campbell, who at 60 had returned to military service to save his family from total deprivation at the hands of the raiders. Commissioned as a captain in the Duke of Argyll's regiment, he was given command of a company of foot, and allowed to remain based at Glenlyon; his company being quartered at Fort William.

The presence of a company of redcoats had dissuaded the raiders, but the damage was already done. Two years before, a group of MacDonald's had raided Glenlyon's tenants at Keppoch, stealing cattle and plundering what little possessions the family still had. The defenceless Campbell's were unable to put up any resistance against the heavily armed highlanders. Discovering a cradle in one of the barns containing a young infant, a raider tipped the baby out, naked, onto the clay floor, and stole the blanket that his mother, Catherine Campbell, had wrapped him in. Her husband, Colin, was the laird's son. This act was seared deeply into the lairds mind.

By the summer of 1691, an uneasy calm had fallen over the highlands. The Privy Council, however, knew that King William had not forgotten them. They awaited the pleasure of the King and dispatched agents south to listen and watch. They did not have a long to wait. After his victory over James in Ireland, the former king had returned to France. His agents reported his army had scattered, and no longer posed a threat. He had spent the summer listening to his advisors and his Queen, who as the daughter of James, was still held in great regard. Occasionally, William would consult his wife on the ways of the English, which he found strange. This was one such occasion.

From his agents in Scotland, unlike Ireland, he was receiving mixed messages. There was still great resentment to William, but no obvious signs of open rebellion. Mary had observed his dilemma and had a suggestion that should consolidate his kingdom without resorting to war.

"My Lord, the Scots are a proud people who long to be independent. It has been so for many generations. My father offered them autonomy, and they believed him, which is why they follow him."

William became visibly annoyed.

"Are you suggesting that I follow your father's offer with one of autonomy, or maybe independence, and split this nation?"

Mary could see his anger, but had a way of calming the impetuous monarch.

"No, my lord, such an offer would endanger this realm and give succour to its enemies. I would counsel that an offer for total amnesty be proclaimed for all Scots Clans involved in the uprising, conditional upon each clan renouncing James, and swearing allegiance to King William."

William nodded and considered Mary's proposal. It was a proposal worth considering. If the clans agreed, then military action would be unnecessary and the treasury would save valuable revenue. Should the Scots refuse the offer, then he would have full justification in destroying them.

The order was drawn up and passed to joint secretary of State for Scotland, John Dalrymple, Second Viscount of Stair, who, in turn, was ordered to present it to the Scots Privy Council.

Back in Glencoe, Annella and her family had settled back into a daily routine, which included the occasional raiding of farms to acquire cattle. Annella, however, did not concern herself with such matters. The Clans were always quarrelling. It was a fine day, and she decided to again climb the Pap. As usual, it took her about 90 minutes. However, today would be different. As she reached the slate covered cap, she saw she was not alone. A young highlander was sitting on a rock gazing out across the loch. He turned as Annella scrambled into view. She recognised him immediately, even without his uniform.

"Donald, what are ya doon here?"

McBane smiled

"Waiting for you bonnie lass, I have something to return to you."

He picked up a long package from the ground, wrapped in hessian cloth.

She smiled and unwrapped it, revealing the basket hilt sword he had picked up at Killiecrankie. Annella studied it for a moment and then sat down. For a few minutes she said nothing, and then she turned to him.

"I know this sword and cannot accept it, Donald. I recognise it. Its former owner was Ian MacDonald. His wife stitched the tartan lining inside the hilt. He was killed fighting with Bonnie Dundee at Killiecrankie pass. I assume you got it there."

Donald nodded.

"I found it on the battlefield. I never saw the owner, but there were several bodies nearby." His voice trailed off as he realised it was not the ideal gift for her.

Annella smiled faintly before replying.

"If I took it and returned it to his wife, she would only ask how I came by it. Awkward questions that I would rather not answer at this time. Keep the sword Donald. It was carried by a true Scottish patriot. You may not have been on the same side, but I see in you the same courage. So, did you kill many of my countrymen that day?"

The question was not unexpected and seemed to be delivered without malice. But it still made Donald uncomfortable, which, of course, was Annella's intention. Donald was not a man to lie or embellish any of his achievements.

"To be truthful, lass, I have no idea. I fired my musket got, chased by highlanders, and had to make an impossible leap for my life over a Burn."

Annella looked at him with wide eyes.

"That was you, Donald? I might have guessed. My father told us of the crazy redcoat who jumped over a 25 foot gap."

She let out a little giggle.

"You are one lucky private, so you are."

Donald smiled back.

"Actually, I'm a sergeant now, but yes, tis lucky I am, but I had no real choice, Lassie. Not if I was to see ye again."

Annella's smile faded and a more serious look came over her face.[i]

She thought for a moment before replying.

"This is a bad time for us, Donald. You're a bonnie lad; make no mistake, but the MacDonalds will nae take kindly to a redcoat courting a MacDonald."

"The war is over, Annella. Scotland and England are united again, the King has stated, he views that the Scots as his loyal subjects. We may have differences, but I am a soldier, I care naught fer politics or politicians. I am a Scot and this is my home."

He stood up and swept his arm out over the mountains of Glencoe that framed the sparkling waters of Loch Leven.

Annella came to him and slipped her hands over his shoulders, looking deeply into his eyes.

"A scot you may be, Donald McBane, but you fight for the English. What if you are ordered to fight me or my family? What would you do then, my bonnie lad?"

Donald looked back into her eyes.

"This."

He said, pulling her close and kissing her full on the lips.

Annella, caught by surprise, stiffened and momentarily pushed back, but then relaxed. She had forgotten what a great kisser he was. Then she returned the kiss with a passion Donald had not felt before. As their lips parted, he said nothing, but gazed deeply into her eyes, searching for her soul. When he finally pulled back, he whispered softly.

"No army, Scots or English, nor the King himself will keep us apart, my bonnie lass."

"Will ye tell that to my father?" She replied with a slight grin.

Donald laughed,

"You think I'm afraid of one MacDonald, remember I faced an entire army of MacDonalds at Killiecrankie."

She laughed out load.

"As I recall, ye nae faced them, ya ran like a rabbit and jumped like one too, so they say."

Donald nodded

"Touché!"

Annella looked puzzled

"Too-chey?"

Donald shook his head.

"It's a French fencing term we use in sword fighting. It means good move, or excellent answer."

"So you speak French now as well?"

She was teasing him now, and he knew it. But no matter. McBane knew that the King had ordered that the Scots clans had been required to sign a pledge of allegiance to King William and his wife Mary. He was unsure of what the MacDonalds response would be and what would happen in the event they refused. Still, that was an unlikely event. The Clans were not stupid. They would grumble and make threats, but would sill sign. Reluctantly maybe, but they would sign.

Chapter 8

The Challenge

Donald and Annella descended the pap together. Upon reaching the lower heather clad slopes, they parted; Annella taking the path back to the village, while Donald made his way to a small clearing where he had tethered his horse. When he arrived, he found a highlander waiting for him; a Maclain MacDonald, by his dress. McBane moved to his horse, nodding in greeting to the stranger and wishing him a good day.

The highlander got to his feet.

"Did ya enjoy the climb, laddie? The view is quite bonny from the top."

McBane turned to face him.

"Have you been spying on me, sir?"

The question made the highlander laugh out loud.

"Spying is it? Well, I am always interested in any man who takes an interest in our girls, especially when that girl is Annella. Macdonald, to put it straight, you're no welcome here Laddie. This is MacDonald land. Take a friendly warning, and nay come back again."

Donald's demeanour changed. He had no wish to cause trouble with the Highlanders in the valley, but was not about to be told what to do by this unwashed bumpkin.

"I have no quarrel with you or the MacDonalds, sir, but I advise you not to threaten me. It may be your undoing."

The Highlander laughed and drew his sword, pointing it towards McBane.

"I can see, Laddie that you are intent on causing trouble here; I think you need a lesson in Highland discipline. If that's a sword ye have wrapped up, ye better arm yourself. I would hate to have to kill a coward."

McBane pulled the blanket from the basket hilt sword and let the cloth drop to the floor. The Highlander saw the MacDonald tartan sash inside the hilt and looked up in surprise.

"Just who the hell are you, Laddie, and where did you get that sword?"

McBane stared at him and replied with purpose and intent.

"Sergeant Donald McBane, Duke of Argyll's regiment of foot, and I got the sword on the field of battle."

"A redcoat in the pay of the usurper William, well I haven't stuck a redcoat since Killiecrankie. This will be a pleasure."

The highlander thrust forward, an action that Donald easily countered; two more slashes met open air as Donald easily deflected them. The Highlanders' frustration became obvious; the redcoat was just playing with him and not taking the combat seriously. He yelled like an enraged bull and began slashing indiscriminately, a panic reaction that Donald was well used to.

He turned and began advancing, his sword hand twisted and turning, clashing with the highlander's weapon a dozen times in less than a minute. The swift attack caught the Highlander off guard. He started to retreat, but Donald's sword was now moving faster than his eyes could follow. The result was a forgone conclusion. Donald's blade slashed across the exposed upper forearm of the panicking highlander. He staggered back, losing his footing and falling backwards. In panic, he reached for his sword, as Donald's boot crushed his wrist, pinning it to the ground. The defeated man now felt the blade touching his throat.

"Yield sir, I have no wish to spill MacDonald blood."

The highlander, surprised to be still alive, nodded slowly.

"Ok Laddie, I yield."

Donald backed away, his sword still levelled at his opponent. He watched for the slightest movement that may signal a treacherous move, but saw none. The highlander slowly got to his feet, carefully and making no attempt to retrieve his weapon.

Donald mounted his horse. As he turned to leave, he addressed the chastened Highlander.

"The war between the scots and the English is over. We are now a united kingdom. I bear no ill will to the Macdonald's, or any Clan, nor to you, sir. We are all Scotsmen now."

The highlander may not have agreed, but was hardly in a position to argue. He watched as McBane rode away. Damn, he thought to himself, if the Redcoats had fought like that at Killiecrankie, he would have been killed along with every other clansman. He smiled softly to himself as he retrieved his sword. Except for that scared rabbit who had run from him and jumped the Burn, of course. *That was one young redcoat that wouldn't have lasted five minutes.*

Chapter 9

Seeds of Destruction

The Secretary of State for Scotland had assembled the Privy Council and had received from King William a despatch that contained the offer of pardon. He now read it aloud. (Actual document on record)

"Suprascribitur William R [1691, Aug. 17.]

Right trustie and entirely beloved Cousine and Councellour, Right trustie and right well beloved Cousines and Councellours, (V. C.) And trustie and well beloved Councellors, We greet yow well.

Whereas we did allow John, Earle of Breadalbin, to meet with the Highlanders and others in armes, in ordor to the reducing of them to our obedience, by a representatione returned in their names, we doe understand their willingness to render themselves in subjectione to our authority and laues, humbly asking our pardone for what is past, and our assistance for accommodating some differences and ffeuds which doe at present, and have verie long trowbled these places. And we being satisfied that nothing can conduce more to the peace of the Highlands, and reduce them, then the taking away the occasion of these differences and feuds which obleidge them to neglect the opportunities to improve and cultivate their countrie, and accustome themselves to depradationes and idleness. Therefore, we are graciouslie pleased, not only to pardon, indemnifie, and restore all that have been in armes, who shall take the oath of alleadgance before the first day of Januarie next. But lykewayes, We are resolved to be at some charge to purchass the lands and superiorities, which are the subject of these debates and animosities, att the full and just avail!, wherby the Highlanders may have their imediat and entire dependence on the croune. And since we are resolved to bestow the expence, and that no bodie is to sustaine any reall prejudice, we must consider it as ill service done to Us and the Countrey, if any concerned shall, through obstinacy or frouardness, obstruct a setlement so advantagious to our service and the publict peace. And we doe expect from yow the outmost applicatione of our *authority to render this designe effectuall; and that yow will communicat our pleasure to the Governour of Innerlochie and other Commandants, that they be exact and dilligent in their severall posts; but that they shew noe more zeall against the Highlanders after their submissione, then they have ever done formerly, when these were in open rebellione. And furder, we doe requyre and authorize yow to emitt a proclamatione, pardoning and indemnifying all that have been in armes against Us and our Government before the first day of Junij last, of all treasones, rebelliones, robbries, depredationes, seditiones, leising—making, hearing and not revealing of treasones: and generally every thing that can be objected against them for being in armes or rebellion preceeding the date of the proclamatione, restoring and reponing all that have been in armes to their lifes, estates, dignities, fame, and blood, as if they had never been guilty, or had never been condemned for the crymes foresaids, as fully and effectually as each of them had particular remissiones, containing a particular enumeratione of their crymes. And that yow expede this indemnity with all convenient dilligence in the accustomed formes, with all clauses ordinary or requisite, without any oyr limitatione or restrictione. But that all such who have been in armes, who may plead the benefite of our gracious indemnity, shall be obleidged to take the oath of alleadgance to Us and our Royall Consort the Queen, betuixt this and the first of January nixt, before yow, or the Shirreffs, or their deputes, of the severall shyres wher they live; and that they subscribe the same by themselves befor witnesses, or by the Shirreffs Clerks for those who cannot wryte. And yow are to require the respective Shirreffs, their Deputes and Clarks, to transmitt to the Clarks of our Privie Councell, exact lists of all persones, by their ordenar designationes, who have subscribed the oath, and taken the benefite of our indemnity, that if any remaine obstinat, they may be prosecute by the severity of the law. We doubt not before this tyme yow have sett Steuart of Appine at liberty, and these who were taken prisoners with hiin, according to the letter from our dearest consort the Queen.* And not doubting of your ready obedience to our pleasure,* *signified to you, in this our letter, which shall be your warrand, we bid yow heartily fareuell.*

Given att our Campt of St. Gerard, the [1]7 of Agust, and of our reigne the third year, by his Majesties command. Sic Subscribitur,"
(The above is copied as recorded)

Dalrymple added that the order from the King was most generous and would ensure peace in Scotland and prevent another war with England. A war they could not hope to win. The Council agreed and unanimously endorsed it for conveyance to the Clans.

The order was greeted with some relief, tinged with concern. Acceptance of the terms would avoid another war with England. The problem was that most highland clans had already pledged allegiance to James.

The order had an expiration date of 1st January, 1692, less than 5 months away.

The Council had to act fast. Agents were immediately dispatched to France to request James release the clans from their oath to allow them to take the oath of allegiance to William. Other Clan chiefs accepted the offer and returned to their councils to consult with clansmen.

The order from the King was received with mixed reactions from the Highland Clans, with the majority accepting the terms. Meanwhile, a bureaucratic system was put in place, allowing for the oath of allegiance to be administered by local magistrates. Among the holdouts was the clan chief Alasdair Maclain, 12th Chief of the MacDonalds of Glencoe. He refused to sign. The chief was a proud man and would not swear allegiance to another king without being released from his oath to King James. So he held back along with others to await James's reply to the Privy Council.

As the summer gave way to autumn, the Highlanders in Glencoe and in other villages throughout the region settled back to an uneasy calm. Talk of the gallant deeds of Bonnie Dundee and the victory of Killiecrankie were common among the taverns and homes of the Clan Maclain. Several naturally mentioned the fleeing redcoat, who jumped to safety across the burn.

The general opinion was that the poor lad was probably still running. In fact, had they only known, the *'poor lad'* in question was at Fort William with his regiment. Annella said nothing, but smiled. Ignorance was bliss. Of course the talk was all hollow. Dundee was dead, his armies beaten, and the redcoat presence in Fort William ensured the Maclains could not even raid the Campbell farms. This suited Annella, of course, as the lull made it easier to contact Donald.

Several of his friends, of course, got to know her, and assisted Donald in keeping the whole affair on a low profile. One of these was a young Lieutenant, Gilbert Kennedy, that McBane had been giving lessons to in fencing and swordplay. Fraternising between officers and other ranks was frowned on, but McBane was in a different category. His skills made him popular with the officers, most of whom had little training in sword fighting, and Sergeant Donald McBane had a reputation for being the best.

Following the King's ultimatum, the Privy Council was convened to ensure the Clans understood the gravity of any refusal to accept the king's terms. The Council called a meeting of the Clans headed by John Campbell, 1st Earl of Breadalbane; and as a member of the Campbell clan, a sworn enemy of the MacDonalds.

Breadalbane had come from Holland where he had been in the audience with the King. He had secured a sum of up to fifteen thousand pounds to use to, in effect, buy off the Clans. Breadalbane's plan was to bribe the chiefs who were yet to sign the Oath, which may have worked; however, the temptation of having such a large sum of money proved too irresistible.

Not a man known for his honesty, the Earl attended the meeting of the clans, and stated that the Government had provided a substantial sum of money to share among the Clans; provided they agreed to sign the document. Of course the Earl did not mention the exact sum, thereby allowing him to keep a large amount for himself. Breadalbane continued in the duplicitous dealings with the Highland chiefs. Stating that he had secured the money but for security reasons it was secure in a chest in London, and would be shared equally among the Clans, once they had come to heel.

Alexander Maclain of the Macdonald's of Glencoe was a man who knew, by personal experience, they could not trust any Campbell.

The Clans had been at each other throats for centuries. They saw the Campbell's lands as rightfully theirs, and no attempt to reach an agreement ever took off. For their part, the Campbells had their loyalty to the King and a legal title to the lands that were not recognised by the Glencoe men.

The uneasy peace between the clans prevailed. Williams's army was camped on the English Scottish border, with orders not to advance on the Highlands while negotiations continued.

As the autumn months moved towards winter, the clans began to drift in and sign the oath, coerced no doubt by the presence of the king's army on the border. However, a hard core still delayed, waiting for James' response from France.

The Privy Council, meanwhile, was growing suspicious of Breadalbane and wrote to him asking where the money he had been allotted had gone and why it had not had the desired effect.

The Earl replied with dismissive curtness,

"The money is spent and the Highlands are quiet and this is the only way of accommodation among friends."

The explanation went a little way to assuring the councilmen, but many suspected that the bulk of the money had been held back from the clans, and remained with Breadalbane, as the most likely scenario.

By December, there were still a number of holdouts. The King, of course, had not visited Scotland, and increasingly relied on his advisors on action taken. Men like Secretary Dalrymple and Earl Breadalbane. Both men had good cause to hate the McLean's of MacDonald in Glencoe. Now they saw the chance to use the King's army to exact the revenge they so earnestly desired.

Most chiefs waited until a reply from the ailing King James finally arrived, giving reluctant consent to the clans' change of allegiance. Not before the Earl of Breadalbane had arranged a private meeting with the Clan chiefs, who still were reluctant to change allegiance. Pointing out that if James were to raise a new army and invade, James would consider their disloyalty an act of treason.

At the meeting, the Earl pledged he had prepared a document reaffirming allegiance to James and signed it. The paper would be kept under close security and only produced should James return. This satisfied the chiefs, and they gave their assent to accept King Williams' offer. Such was the way of politics in 1691.

The Privy Council moved fast and by December 20th all but the Glencoe men had attended and signed. Realising the futility of withstanding the order, Chief Alexander Maclain of Glencoe left for Fort William with a small escort of highlanders. The Old Fox, as the Campbells had dubbed him, was 62 years old, and to make matters worse, he had commenced his journey as a heavy snowstorm swept the region.

On the 31st of December, Colonel Hill at Fort William was advised that the Clan chief of MacDonald was seeking an audience with him. Hill immediately consented, and in minutes the Chief and his escorting clansmen stood before him.

He immediately ordered whisky to be brought and bid them sit, and enquired what they wanted.

The Chief stood up.

"As ye are aware, King James has released us from our pledge ta him. We have agreed that the proper course of action is to accept the King William's offer and have come to take the oath."

Hill said nothing for a moment before replying.

"I cannot accept your oath Alexander; the oaths must be sworn before a magistrate to be acceptable under the terms. You will need to go to the sheriff at Inveraray, who can accept the oath."

To the Chief this seemed an impossible task. Inveraray was over 70 miles south and heavy snow was sweeping the region. Colonel Hill sympathised but was powerless to act. Instead, he offered to pen a letter to The Sheriff, stating that the Clan had made the deadline when they reached Fort William, but because of the severe weather, it was impossible for him to make the journey to the Sheriff in time. He requested the oath be administered and forwarded to the Privy Council requesting the King to accept it, and thus protect the Clan from any punishment, in that they had endeavoured to comply with the terms. After writing, Hill put down his quill and dusted the document with powder, before offering it to the Chief.

"Here you are Alex; that is the best I can do. Haste you ta Inveraray and present the letter to Sir Colin Campbell."

The Chief accepted the letter, and after thanking Hill for his hospitality, left the Fort and headed south. The weather was not too pleasant, but the old man and his party strove on through the cold and light snow. His companions pointed out, the journey would take them within a mile of Glencoe and suggested they call at the chief's home to refresh themselves and get dry. The old chief would have none of it.

"I'm nae gong ta take a break on such an important mission. The safety of all of us at Glencoe depends on the King's acceptance of the oath. None ill say that Alasdair Maclain MacDonald ever put the clan in danger."

The journey took two days, but on arrival, Sir Colin Campbell, the Magistrate was not in residence. He was away visiting his family.

The chief and his attendants, with no other choice, waited, and on January 6th the sheriff arrived. He received the delegation, but Like Colonel Hill, stated that the deadline had passed. Therefore, taking the oath would have no validity. There is little doubt that Sir John was well pleased that the MacDonalds had delayed too long. He now saw a bona fide reason to use the army to rid himself once and for all from the troublesome clan.

The chief pointed out that he had arrived at Fort William the day before the deadline, following advice that the Governor was the man he needed to consult. When told the advice was wrong, he did all he could to reach Inveraray in time.

The sheriff was unmoved, insisting that Alexander had ample time to reach him after the Privy council had relayed the message from King James. This was of course true, but the Sherriff was also aware of the rider put on the King's order; that late signers should be shown mercy and details passed to the King for his decision.

For some time, the chief pleaded with Campbell and finally reduced to tears; he stated he was prepared to lodge an appeal direct to the Privy Council if the sheriff declined to act.

This left Campbell in a dilemma. If he accepted the oath, and passed the matter to the King, he risked the wrath of Secretary Dalrymple and Livingstone, who clearly wanted the clan erased, under the guise of treason, to the King. If however he refused and the Chief protested to the Council, or even the King himself, then he could be accused of failing to comply with the Kings directive that latecomers would be able to appeal to the king if circumstances made it impossible to sign in time. That would also be an act of treason.

Finally, the Sheriff decided to administer the oath and pass it to the Council along with Colonel Hill's letter. A much relieved chief thanked him for his assistance and began the slow journey back to Glencoe.

Meanwhile, Secretary Dalrymple had noted with satisfaction that the Maclains had held back on the signing. He penned a letter on the matter to Sir Thomas Livingstone, commander of the English forces in Scotland.

(Copied as record on file)

"11th January 1692

To Sir Thomas Livingstone

Now that the time for taking the oath of Allegiance has expired you are instructed to march the troops against the rebels who had not taken the benefit of the indemnity, and to destroy them by fire and sword;" but lest such a course might render them desperate, you are allowed to "give terms and quarters, but in this manner only, that chieftains and heritors, or leaders, be prisoners of war, their lives only safe, and all other things in mercy, they taking the oath of allegiance, and rendering their arms, and submitting to the government, are to have quarters, and indemnity for their lives and fortunes, and to be protected from the soldiers."

Signed

Dalrymple

Secretary of state for Scotland"

The letter was countersigned by the King.

As a PostScript, the Secretary added a note with the order which read.

"I have no great kindness to Keppoch nor Glencoe, and it is well that people are in mercy, and then just now my Lord Argyle tells me that Glencoe hath not taken the oath, at which I rejoice. It is a great work of charity to be exact in rooting out that damnable sect, the worst of the Highlands."

To say that Livingstone was perplexed would be an understatement. From the letter, it seemed that although the king was prepared to entertain mercy for the Clan MacDonald, the Secretary of State was not. It seemed as if the MacDonalds had been singled out.

He queried the order, and on the 16th of January, received a reply from Dalrymple.

The letter stated

"The king does not at all incline to receive any after the diet but in mercy but for a just example of vengeance, I entreat the thieving tribe of Glencoe may be rooted out to purpose."

In order to make his wishes clear, duplicate letters were also sent to Colonel Hill, the governor of Fort William, with the letter of an import similar to that sent to Livingston. From the following extract, it would appear that not only the Earl of Breadalbane but also the Earl of Argyle, was privy to this infamous transaction.

"The Earls of Argyle and Breadalbane have promised that they shall have no retreat in their bounds, the passes to Rannoch would be secured, and the hazard certified to the land of Weems to reset them; in that case, Argyle's detachment with a party that may be posted in Island Stalker must cut them off."

Colonel Hill was uneasy at this development. True, the MacDonalds had signed late, but there was good reason for the delay.

The Governor was aware that Maclain had arrived on the 31st, but had to travel onwards in heavy weather to reach the Magistrates' Office, only to find him away for the New Year. He was bound by duty to take preparatory action. He forwarded the order to move a detachment of the Argyll's regiment of foot to relocate to Glencoe.

Knowing that Sir Colin Campbell had forwarded MacDonald's oath and the accompanying letter to the Privy Council, Hill felt he could safely assume that the matter would be sent to the King for his decision. In fact, this had not been the case, even though all the oaths were duly recorded, having been received on the same day, all on the same paper, and all from the Sheriff. The Privy Council noted that the Maclain oath had a date of 6th January. After some debate, the council determined they could not accept the oath without a royal warrant from the king.

The Earl of Argyll, Sir Colin Campbell, however, well knew the king was a fair man and may well grant the Maclains mercy in this disposition. The Earl was well aware of the desire among the army hierarchy that the MacDonald problem be dealt with. He had no wish to go against the wishes of the Secretary and Sir Thomas Livingstone. So, he made a fateful decision.

Sir Colin did not forward the documents as might be expected. He separated the MacDonald oath from the rest and put it aside. He glanced around the room, noting the other council members were deep in conversation, and paying little attention. He whispered softly to himself,

"You had enough time to sign when it mattered. Now your fate is sealed." He inscribed the paper, Delete and Obliterate. Best to keep the King out of the loop; by this one act of duplicity, the fate of the MacDonalds of Glencoe had been sealed.

Chapter 10

Prelude to a Massacre

The village of Glencoe was in fact 3 separate settlements comprising the small hamlets of Auchendean, Invercoe, and Inveriggan. It lay in the shadow of a four thousand foot mountain known as the Pap. The entrance to the glen was faced by the tranquil waters of Loch Leven. It was towards this picturesque scene that a detachment of 120 redcoat troops was now moving.

The winter had coated the village with snow, and log and peat homes took on a picturesque Christmas like scene with blue smoke wisping from the granite chimneys. Wrapped in a thick woollen shawl, Annella was fetching water from the well, when her attention was drawn to the snow covered road leading out of the Glen and around the waters of Loch Leven, towards Ballachulish House and Fort William.

About a mile distant, she could see a detachment of redcoats approaching the village. She could not identify them, but noted at least 3 were mounted on horseback. This was a large party, and more than a little suspicious. Quickly, Annella returned to her house, and together with her father, and then went to the Chief's dwelling. Quickly, the chief directed his son, John, to gather what men he could and to find out the redcoats intent.

Captain Robert Campbell of Glenlyon was not a young man. At 60 years, he had a reputation for drinking and being bad tempered. He had been forced to re-join the King's army to pay for his, not inconsiderable, gambling debts, and to allow the Argyll's regiment to assign a company to him as protection from the MacDonald's raids. Despite the animosity between the Clans, Roberts's niece was married to the chief's son, Alexander. She was also the sister of the infamous outlaw, Rob Roy Macgregor, who was a popular folk hero among the Highlands. This made him part of the Macdonald's family, at least in their eyes.

As Captain Campbell approached the village, he saw a party of about 20 armed highlanders waiting for him. He called a halt to the column and rode forward with two junior officers. John recognised the captain remained impassive, his men blocking the road. He addressed Campbell.

"Good day Robert, what is the purpose of you bringing such a large force to our peaceful village? You have no enemies here."

Campbell smiled

"Nor do we, John. I have been assigned to find suitable quarters to enable us to collect arrears of cess and hearth money, a relatively new tax imposed by the Scottish parliament. Mr Lindsey, the order, if you please."

The Lieutenant handed a despatch to Campbell, who in turn, handed it to the Chief's son. The order was signed by Col. Hill. After reading the order, he handed it back and extended his hand.

"You are most Welcome Robert. Alex and his wife will be glad to see you. We will see to the quartering of your lads here."

The highlanders parted from the road and shouted welcomes to the soldiers, whose breath was rapidly condensing to vapour in the keen highland air. The effects of the cold were showing on their faces. They seemed pleased that they would soon find shelter from the bite of winter.

Annella quickly spotted a familiar face among the soldiers. Gilbert Kennedy was securing his horse when she came up.

"Well, Gilbert, I hear you and the others are looking for a place to stay. We have plenty of room here, and I know Donald would want me to look after you."

Kennedy smiled and removed his hat.

"Well, thank you Miss Macdonald, I would be delighted. Do you have room for Mr Farquhar here? He is a good friend, and I hate to leave him at the tender mercies of your womenfolk."

Annella smiled.

"Now we can't have that, can we? Of course, you are both welcome. Come in and warm yourselves."

Within 2 hours, the column had moved into the dwellings of Glencoe, spreading out among the three small hamlets that populated the Glen. The following day, the snow had cleared, and Gilbert and Farquhar asked Annella to accompany them while they took a walk through the Glen. She readily accepted, telling her father that what girl could refuse the company of such gallant gentlemen.

The snow covered ground sparkled with an almost sterile whiteness in the bright morning sun, and the air was crisp and clean. Towering over the village was the magnificent Pap of Glencoe, a two and a half thousand foot peak that was normally topped with a grey slate cap. This morning the cap was a brilliant white while the mountain stood dark and forbidding, its snow swept sides were streaked with driven snow. The sight was breath taking.

Gilbert gazed at it before commenting.

"So, that's the Pap. Donald told me you and he often climb it in the summer."

Annella smiled. *"True enough, but it's a pretty stiff climb. In the winter, it would tax the strongest man."*

Gilbert smiled.

"Only a fool would go mountain climbing at this time of the year. But maybe soldiers are fools, right?"

He looked back at the mountain and shook his head.

Over the next few days, the soldiers settled in with the MacDonalds. Some of the younger girls seemed quite taken with the youthful soldiers, who were more than happy to return the favours. It soon became apparent that most of the troops were not Campbell's; they came from the lowlands and other areas.

Of course, Annella was disappointed that Donald was not with the detachment but was most interested in news of Donald, who had been posted to duty with the King's army in the Netherlands.

Disappointingly, Gilbert had not heard from him lately, but knew that the fighting had died down and that he was most probably filling his time by giving fencing lessons to incompetent officers. Annella smiled at the news.

It was several days later that a messenger arrived from Fort William with a missive addressed to Captain Robert Campbell of Glenlyon and sealed with the red wax seal. In the privacy of his office, Glenlyon opened the order.

(Actual Document on record)

You are hereby ordered to fall upon the rebells, the MacDonalds of Glenco, and put all to the sword under seventy. You are to have a speciall care that the old Fox and his sones doe upon no account escape your hands, you are to secure all the avenues that no man escape. This you are to putt in execution att fyve of the clock precisely; and by that time, or very shortly after it, I'll strive to be att you with a stronger party: if I doe not come to you att fyve, you are not to tarry for me, but to fall on. This is by the Kings speciall command, for the good & safety of the Country, that these miscreants be cutt off root and branch. See that this be putt in execution without feud or favour, else you may expect to be dealt with as one not true to King nor Government, nor a man fitt to carry Commissione in the Kings service. Expecting you will not faill in the full-filling hereof, as you love your selfe, I subscribe these with my hand att Balicholis Feb: 12, 1692.

For their Majesties service
(signed) R. Duncanson
To Capt.
Robert Campbell
of Glenlyon

Campbell said nothing but folded up the order and placed it in his tunic. Time had run out for the MacDonalds.

****

On the 12th of February, Annella spotted Gilbert and Lieutenant Farquhar standing near the trail that led to Inveriggan; both seemed subdued, and they stopped talking as Annella approached.

"Well Gilbert, such a long face, have I done something to upset you?"

He shot a glance at Farquhar before replying.

"Nothing really, Annella. Just soldierly complaints. Let's go for a walk."

Farquhar shot him a warning look, but it was ignored by Gilbert, and went unnoticed by Annella. The two walked away. Despite Gilbert's attempts at normality, Annella realised that something was not right. Although she barely knew him, she had already become a shrewd judge of men. After about a quarter of a mile, she stopped and turned to him.

"Alright Gilbert, your friend is out of the way. Can you tell me what's the matter? You look like a man who has lost his dog and given up hope."

Gilbert turned to her, seemed about to say something, then quickly turned away, scanning his surroundings, as if looking for the answer.

Finally, He looked down at the stream bubbling out of the hillside and selected a smooth rock. Without looking at Annella, he addressed the rock.

"Mighty rock of Glencoe, you have lain here since time itself began. No man can ever deny your absolute right to be here, nor should they. But if I could suggest that tonight you do not tarry in this place, tonight you roll elsewhere."

He stood up and dropped the rock into the flowing stream, and it immediately began to roll downstream, propelled by the current. It was almost as if the rock had heard him. He stood up and looked intently at Annella.

Her demeanour had changed and a white pallor had flushed her face. The cryptic message had been received. Gilbert turned away and walked slowly back along the Glen. Farquhar was waiting.

"Did you tell her, Gilbert?" he enquired.

Gilbert shook his head.

"No, but I hope to God she got my message."

Farquhar replied, *"So what do you intend to do? If the rumour is true, this is murder under trust, pure and simple; the regiment will be dammed for all eternity."*

Gilbert looked back up the glen.

"Damn the bloody regiment. I will not kill helpless civilians, and certainly not for some damn Campbell vendetta."

Farquhar tried to sound reassuring.

"No need to worry yet. You know how the rumour mill works. We will probably be sent back to Fort William in a couple of days. One thing for sure, is that if they were planning to turn on the MacDonalds, then we would have done it by now. The Captain is missing good drinking time, and you know how he misses his drink?"

Gilbert nodded, but neither man seemed too convinced.

Three-hundred yards away, Annella stood in shock, replaying gilberts, words in her mind, then she gasped under a low breath.

"Oh, my God! No."

She quickly hurried back to her house, trying not to run and therefore attract attention. Elsewhere in the Glen, unease was spreading among the billeted troops. Up till now, there had been just a suspicion that the troops would be ordered to kill their hosts. Now, the orders to assemble with full kit at 5 am left them in little doubt what their mission was to be. Like Gilbert, many found ways to give surreptitious clues to warn their hosts.

As the house settled down in front of the fire, one such soldier admired the weave on his hosts' plaid. He complimented the workmanship, and was told the man's wife was the seamstress. He then asked if he could examine it. His host duly handed it over. The soldier ran the material through his hands,

"It is a fine piece of work, sir. If this Plaid was mine, I would put it over my shoulders, and go this very night to check on my cattle, and I would

take my family along to keep me company; and then to a safe place to keep them from the foul night."

And gave a sombre nod to his host.

He handed back the garment. His host quickly exchanged glances with the other family members before replying slowly and deliberately.

"Thank you, sir, for that suggestion. I may well take it up."

A look of relief came over the redcoat's face.

"Well sir, on that note, I will turn in if I may. But please carry on with your conversations. I am a heavy sleeper, and I assure you, will not disturb me."

He stood up and moved into his room. For 20 minutes he lay on his bed, before he heard the family gathering clothing and getting ready to leave. He smiled softly to himself as he heard the back door close. After a few minutes, he quietly arose and checked the rooms. The house was deserted.

"God speed my friends."

He whispered under his breath.

At around the same time, another family was alerted, when the soldier billeted with them began talking to their dog, suggesting it would be safer tonight if he would make his bed in the heather. By 1 am, several families had received similar warnings, and had left their homes. But tragically many more received no warning at all.

Chapter 11

Massacre

The evening was winding down. Captain Robert Campbell had enjoyed the company of the chief's sons, John, and Alexander; they had played several rounds of cards. The sound of bagpipes cut through the crisp night air outside while the snow again began to blow around the house. The piper was none other than Hugh McKenzie, piper to Captain Campbell. He stood atop the Henderson stone, just below the road. Seemingly oblivious to the weather, John Maclain remarked to his guest.

"Hugh seems to have had a wee dram too many Robert; this is no weather to practise the pipes. Fine though they are, mind ye."

The captain did not reply. But Hugh was neither drunk nor practicing. The cold meant little to him, but the lament he played, however, did. The 'Women of the Glen', was a traditional Scottish lament. People often played it as a warning of grave misfortune. Hugh had hoped that there were some members tucked in the warm this night, would hear, and heed it.

Elsewhere in the village, the lament was heard, and some of the already suspicious Macdonald's decided it may be time to move. Others noticed that while everyone else was seeking shelter, the Soldiers were still in uniform, and were apparently on alert.

The night wore down, and it was late when the Captain left; thanking Alex and John, as well as his niece, Jean Macdonald, for their hospitality. John bade him goodnight, but not before he extended his hand.

"Good night to ye Robert, there is a storm blowing in. I trust ye will grace our house tomorrow for dinner after your duties."

"Thank you John, I would be most happy to accept. Sleep well friend, we will talk more tomorrow."

The Captain smiled good-naturedly as he left; fully aware that in his tunic pocket, he had the orders from Col Hill to murder both Alex, John, and his niece in the early hours.

Robert, however, did not go home. As the unsuspecting MacDonalds retired for the night, he was very much awake. As secrecy and stealth, was of the utmost importance, Captain Campbell had planned his attack with ruthless military precision. He divided his force into three separate units. The operation was to commence simultaneously at five am. The sleeping families were to receive no warning and no chance to defend themselves.

At this order, two officers stepped forward. Gibson and Farquhar had listened to the order. It was Gibson who spoke first.

"No sir, I will not commit cold blooded murder on families who have shown me nothing but kindness."

Donaldson almost exploded with rage.

"Lieutenant Gibson, you will obey orders. Is that clear, sir?"

Gibson glared insolently at the shaking officer. He slowly drew his sword and broke the blade over his knee.

"I will not sir, damn your orders, and damn the consequences."

Before the startled officer could reply, Farquhar also drew his sword and broke it in a similar fashion.

"I agree with Lieutenant Gibson, Captain. I am an officer in the King's army, and I will not dishonour my name or regiment. Murder under trust if you must, but you do it without us."

Both officers saluted and stared at the two captains.

Barely able to control himself, Donaldson approached the two men.

"Officers, you think you are, well I say you are both snivelling craven cowards, a disgrace to your regiment and your families. Mr Lyndsey, sir, place these two rebel lovers under close arrest, put them in chains, and have them escorted To Ballachulish."

Lyndsey saluted and detailed two men to take charge of the prisoners.

Meanwhile, the heavy snow had slowed the approach of Lieutenant Colonel Hamilton in command of 400 extra troops out from Fort William. The detachment halted in the face of worsening conditions, some 3 miles from the entrance to Glencoe.

Hamilton was well aware that Captain Campbell had been ordered to begin the attack on the villagers at 5 am. He had good reason to delay. The population consisted of around 200 sleeping villagers, against a detachment of fully armed troops, from the Argyll's regiment of foot.

"Sir, if we are to make Glencoe by 7 am, we should be leaving soon, especially in this weather."

The voice of his aide broke into Hamilton's thoughts.

He turned to the Major.

"Tell me, Major, what do the men feel about this operation? Truthfully?"

The Major knew exactly what they thought, but was unsure of what to say, so he chose his words carefully.

"Well Sir, it's a bloody business, there's no denying. The men will obey orders, of course, but, well, they're not happy about it, that's a fact."

Hamilton nodded; the men were all Highlanders, mostly Scottish born. They were aware that the actions planned would be taken as murder under trust, a heinous crime that could never be forgiven. He smiled before replying.

"Well, I intend to keep the men here until it's light and the blizzard blows through. Captain Campbell will move against the Rebels at 5 o'clock. I anticipate the matter will be resolved by then. Our orders were to be in position at 7 to secure the escape routes. The Secretary made that abundantly clear. However, the Secretary did not anticipate the weather. I am sure Captain Campbell is more than capable of dealing with this

problem, thus, I feel the men would be happy for the delay. Do you not think so, Major?"

The major smiled to himself. This could turn out well after all. Any repercussions would be on Campbell of Glenlyon's head, a drunken old man who had a grudge to settle with the MacDonalds, anyway. His men would not be present, so could not be accused.

He saluted and replied,

"I think we will have a most successful outcome, sir."

Elsewhere in the village, John Maclain and his brother Sandy were asleep, when he was awoken by voices outside his home, calling his name. From his bed, he could hear the wind and snow buffeting the house.

"Someone must be crazy," he muttered under his breath.

Glancing out of the window, he could see little, and when he opened the door, the men, who were soldiers, had drifted away. Sandy, still sleepy, made some comment about drunken soldiers who had nothing better to do but wake their hosts with pranks, though John was not that sure. This was a strange hour to be afoot in the village, and clearly the dress of the soldiers appeared to be full field kit.

A sudden dread came over him. His father had signed the oath late. The Privy Council had nonetheless accepted it, and, coincidently, a company of redcoats was billeted in the town, ostensibly to collect taxes. Yet, as John's servant pointed out, there had been little attempt to do so.

He got dressed and decided to investigate further. He followed the soldiers to the hamlet of Inveriggan. On his approach, it was obvious the entire company was being assembled. The company was turned out in full battle order and was being addressed by Robert himself. On seeing the two brothers, Robert turned and approached them. John spoke first;

"This seems an odd time for military manoeuvres Robert, are you planning harm to your hosts? Should we be concerned?"

John and Sandy were both wearing their swords, and John was resting his left hand on its scabbard. The movement was not lost on the Captain; who considered taking both men now? But any shot would have clearly aroused the sleeping Macdonald s. Likewise, any attempt at swordplay would surely lead to noise and shouts that would likely have the same effect. The Captain smiled with no hint of the malevolence in his heart.

"Don't worry yourself John, the Macdonald are quite safe. We have orders to move against the Glengarry men who are causing unrest. It's a long march so we need to set off early. Do you really think that if any harm was intended to you I would allow you and Sandy, no to mention Jean, my niece, to remain here? Your fears are groundless, my friend. Now haste ye back to your home. We are paid to brave this weather; you can rest easy in your beds. I'll see you tomorrow, friend."

John relaxed and bade the captain good night. The three men returned home, but although he was reassured, the same could not be said for William Simpson, his servant. He had a mistrust of the Redcoats and had fought them at Killiecrankie.

John noticed his discomfort.

"You seem troubled, Will; do you no believe Captain Robert?"

William shook his head.

"I dinna trust the man sir, he's a Campbell and they have na love for you or your father, and I could see nay sign of Macdonald of Inveriggan. The Captain had been living with him for two weeks. Should the Chief not have been there to see him off? Something is wrong here. If ya dinna mind, sir, 'll sit up a spell."

John laughed.

"Aye Will, stay up and watch. I will be away ta me bed friend, Sandy too, I'd wager."

His brother smiled and nodded before taking a quick look outside. He saw little but falling snow.

Campbell and his men had, by this time, finished their briefing, and the men were moving quietly to their assigned stations.

John and Sandy quickly returned to their still warm beds and soon drifted off. Meanwhile, Captain Campbell and his men began the final perpetration of the operation. Lieutenant Lyndsey was dispatched to the home of the MacDonald Chief with a company of 20 troops, his orders; to eliminate the chief and his family.

Inside the home where he had been billeted, his host, Macdonald of Inveriggan, was bound and gagged along with other members of the household. In his pocket, the chief still had the letter of protection, signed by Colonel Hill, personally. It was to no avail. They all knew they had not long to live. In fact, the only reason they were still alive was that the rest of the valley was sleeping, blissfully unaware of the impending horror that stalked them. Campbell needed to keep it that way. He waited for Lyndsey to get in position.

The house of the Clan chief was in darkness as the party led by Lyndsey approached. Captain Campbell had made it plain to him that the old chief was the main target. He had to die, and no excuses would be tolerated should he escape. Lyndsey had decided on the strategy. He walked up to the door and knocked firmly. After a few moments, a light appeared, obviously from a candle. Lyndsey waited. A servant opened the door. Lyndsey bowed slightly to the sleepy man and said.

"My apologies for calling at this hour. Can you inform the Chief, that I have some urgent business with him that needs his immediate attention?"

The servant nodded and walked back into the house. Outside, Lyndsey fingered his pistol nervously. From down the road came a sudden musket shot, muted by the worsening weather. Fog had rolled in with the snowstorm and the temperature was dropping fast. Both the Chief and his wife were fast asleep when he was awoken by the servant.

"My apologies sir, there is an Argyll officer outside who says he has to see you urgently."

Alexander opened his eyes and lifted his head from the pillow. It took a second or two for the words to register.

"Well, invite the fellow in, it's too foul a night to be left in the cold. Tell him I will be there directly."

It was the last words Maclain would utter. He started to rise from the bed; as his servant turned towards the door to be confronted by Lyndsey, pistol drawn.

The Chief was half out of bed when the officer levelled his pistol and fired. His servant lunged for the officer's pistol, but it was too late. The shot Struck Maclain high in the upper chest. Two soldiers then entered with muskets drawn. Both fired simultaneously. One shot struck Maclain a second time, throwing him back in a shower of blood. His wife screamed and caught him as he fell. The second musket shot was aimed at her, but struck Maclain's servant as he threw himself forward to protect her.

His body crashed into Maclain's wife as she cradled the head of her dying husband.

Satisfied that Maclain was dead, Lyndsey turned and left the house, ignoring the screams of his wife, as the soldiers tore her clothes off and fell upon her like a pack of wild dogs, laughing.

One grabbed her hand after seeing her gold wedding ring. He tried to wrench the ring free.

"You won't be needing this anymore, you old whore."

He yelled at the screaming woman. Finally, he used his teeth to wrench the ring free. Throughout the house, sounds of smashing doors and looting drowned out the unfortunate woman's screams. Lyndsey watched the carnage unfolding around him. Several houses were now burning. In the flickering light from the fires, the laughing soldiers dragged out of the house Mrs Maclain's naked body. She was battered and bleeding, but still breathing. They dragged her into the snow and left her there. But not before one of them stamped repeatedly on her breasts before walking away.

The unfortunate woman lay there, too weak to get up. Then the soldiers left. She lay there, staring up at the blizzard of falling snow. Strangely, she felt little pain. The numbing cold slowly crept over her body. Tears filled her eyes, not for herself but for her slain husband, and most likely her entire family. She died there alone several hours later of exposure, long after the soldiers left the now deserted village on fire.

****

William scanned the road leading up towards Inveriggan. The snow had eased slightly. Faintly, he heard the sound of feet crunching through snow. Pulling his cloak up around his neck, he moved quietly, and quickly, from the house, taking care to remain in the shadows. The noise grew more distinct. By the half-light from the snow covered ground, he saw them; Soldiers, moving slowly, and in loose formation, their fixed bayonets glistening in the moonlight. They were not moving out towards Glengarry. They were approaching the hamlet, and William quickly guessed their intended target. He hurried back to the house and quickly roused John and Sandy.

"Sir, we must leave now. Redcoat soldiers are coming, all armed with muskets. We are betrayed, sir."

John did not question his servant or hesitate, other than to ask,

"How long before they get here?"

"A few minutes, at most."

From the house, they heard gunfire. It was coming from the Chief's house, about half a mile distant.

John quickly roused Sandy and his family, including Campbell's niece. Grabbing what blankets and clothes they could, they made their exit from the rear of the house, John and Sandy - grabbing a sword each,

72

on the way. Their escape was well under way when a servant from the Chief's house stumbled out of the blizzard.

The elderly man had escaped the carnage, possibly due to his age, but his warning only confirmed what William had told them.

"Flee quickly; there is no time for resting, when your father lies murdered at the hands of the redcoats."

The exhausted man fell, gasping, to his knees. John and Sandy quickly ushered the women and servants out of the back door. Almost as soon as they got clear, the redcoats reached the house, fanning out and surrounding it. A burley trooper kicked in the door, and a handful of troops burst inside, swiftly searching the house and overturning beds. A young officer with the detail walked through the house, and on exiting the back door, saw the trail of footprints in the snow leading into the darkness; the snow storm was already rapidly covering them.

"Shall we follow them, sir?" A young private enquired.

The officer considered briefly, but to do so would split his force. And maybe alert others.

"No, they will keep for now, burn the house and fan out, kill everyone you find, no exceptions, no mercy. The Captain wants them all dead."

John and his family moved quickly, heading uphill, away from the carnage, into the hills above Auchendean, the rugged bluffs that may provide some shelter. Then they heard the musket shots and screams coming from Inveriggan.

In the darkness, two or three figures moved. John saw the glint of unsheathed swords. He drew his sword and moved with his brother in front of his family.

The figures came closer, and to his relief, he could see they were not soldiers.

Annella spoke first.

"John, Thank God, I thought you were dead, they're killing everybody."

The Chief's son caught her as she rushed forward.

"Aye Lass, the murdering Campbell scum. My father put his trust in them, and I fear he has not survived."

Annella embraced John, tears filling her eyes.

"We would have been dead too, all of us, but for two of Donald's friends who warned us. I fear they will pay a high price if they were seen."

Down in the hamlet, Campbell had ordered the bound men, dragged from the house that he had shared with them for the last few days. The men were thrown to the ground in front of him, as redcoats moved among them, shooting each man in the head as they struggled to sit up.

A young man of around nineteen or twenty stood in terror, staring at Campbell. The captain drew his sword and levelled it at the youth, but stayed his hand as the youth began praying. He was interrupted by Captain Thomas Drummond, who yelled at Campbell.

"Why is this rebel still alive? No Prisoners Captain, No prisoners."

He slashed down with his sword, striking the youth across the neck, almost decapitating him. The boy's body fell sideways, blood pumping from his severed jugular, and spreading into the fresh snow, making an ugly melted puddle. At this, a young boy of around 12 rushed forward and fell to his knees before Campbell.

"Please, Sir, don't kill me. I will be your servant and do whatever you ask of me. I don't want to die."

Campbell paused, and a flicker of compassion crossed his face. He stared at the upturned young face as blood suddenly erupted from his mouth, cutting off his pleas. Drummond had plunged his dirk into the boy's back, thrusting it up so the point burst through his chest.

"That's how we deal with thieving rebel scum, Captain."

Drummond laughed and turned away.

Now, screams were filling the Hamlet. The redcoats began smashing in front doors, and firing parties were formed outside the buildings. Men, women, and children were spilling out of the houses, and were being shot at by the Redcoat soldiers. Most of the people were barely dressed, wrapped in blankets. The storm and blowing snow gave them some cover. The Soldiers' muskets were not known for their accuracy, but even allowing for that, they missed their mark with most shots. Some of the balls, smashing through tree branches several feet above the fleeing villagers. It appeared as if the soldiers were deliberately shooting wide, a fact that must have been obvious to their officers.

However, not all were so disposed; one of the soldiers from Campbell's own regiment had not forgotten the deprivations committed by the MacDonalds in the past. As he gleefully thrust his blade into a luckless and screaming victim, he yelled,

"That's for Catharine's Blanket, and that's for Colin's cows."

Like the MacDonald's, the Campbell's had long memories.

Up in the Hamlet of Auchendean, a third squad of redcoats, under the command of Sergeant Barbour, surprised a party of nine clansmen sitting in front of the fire. Among the party was the Laird of Auchendean, who was aware of the gunfire elsewhere in the Glen, but confident that he was in no danger. Well aware that in his pocket, he carried a protection order signed personally by Colonel Hill.

It was of little use. Barbour and his men opened fire on the party immediately upon entering the house. The Laird died instantly, along with 4 others in the party. The rest of the party fled the house, via the back door, some suffering gunshot wounds of varying degrees. One, however, was seized by Baker. He was the Laird's brother; whom Barbour had been sharing the house with for the past two weeks. He stood defiantly as Barbour pushed him against a wall, and three soldiers took aim at him. With what was to have been his last words, the Scot addressed his would be killer.

"Barbour, If I am to die, let it not be in my own home here, where we lived as friends; But outside, with my kinfolk."

Barbour replied.

"In consideration of your hospitality, and the fact that I have eaten of your bread and meat, I will grant that request."

The Highlander picked up his Plaid, throwing it loosely over his shoulder. The firing party of 4 men loaded their muskets and stepped outside where they formed up, and as he reached the party, offered some them some advice.

"Shoot straight Laddies, I dinna want to go slow."

He did not wait for a reply. With one hand, he swept the plaid from his shoulder and cast it like a net over the unsuspecting firing party. Then, pushing Barbour aside, he ran for the side of the building, quickly disappearing in the blinding snow, before the soldiers could free themselves from the plaid.

Barbour watched him, his host; go off into the night, a slight smile on his face. At least he would not have the death of this Macdonald on his conscience.

It was, however, of little consequence. Throughout the hamlet, the residents were spilling out from the houses, most in a state of undress. A scene repeated in the other two hamlets. They moved out into the snow lashed darkness, desperately trying to escape the carnage. The soldiers fired at the fleeing villages, but most shots, either by accident or design, passed harmlessly over the villager's heads. This was a vain gesture. Crying children clung to their mothers, who stumbled and slipped on the frozen ground. Over half would perish that night as the snow, robbing their bodies of heat. They died alone. Curled up in the snow

Mothers, their arms wrapped around the infants, stayed with the infants who drifted off to sleep, never to awaken again. Their mothers, too weak to rise, followed them into death.

The exact number who died of exposure that night could never be calculated. Estimates put it at least 100 souls.

Chapter 12

Aftermath

The Blizzard subsided overnight and dawn brought a scene of absolute horror. In the tranquil glen, bodies lay where they had fallen. Among a pile of frozen corpses outside a burnt cottage, the severed hand of an infant child, no doubt caught up in the bloodlust of the soldiers. Some houses still smouldered. A few that had been abandoned still stood, providing some shelter for the soldiers who had carried out the killings.

By 11 am, the main party of Hamilton's troops arrived, four hundred (400) members of the Argyll regiment, belatedly taking up position to secure the crossing points and exits from the glen. By which time there was no one left alive to flee. Hamilton surveyed the scene, as Major Donaldson and his party, including Campbell, appeared from the devastation. Donaldson saluted.

"Good morning, sir. We have cleared out the rebels. Those that were not killed have fled into the snow and mountains without clothing or shelter. They will not last the day."

Hamilton looked around the smoking ruins, then back at Campbell.

"Mister Campbell, do you have a final body count?"

"We have 38 bodies, mostly male, but including some women and children. Several families fled before the attack. The old fox is among the dead; unfortunately his sons were not in their house when we burned it."

Hamilton thought for a moment. This was hardly the news the secretary was expecting. If there were survivors, then they would be able to tell of the massacre, and of the way it was carried out. Murder under trust was a crime that no highlander would tolerate. Of course, he had the signed king's order in his possession, so no blame would be attached to him and his men, surely. They were obeying the kings' orders. If there was any blame, it rested on his Majesty's shoulders.

Finally, he looked back at Campbell and Donaldson.

"Search the village again, kill anyone you find left alive, and burn every house. We ensure that there is nothing here for these rebels to return to."

The soldiers with loaded muskets fanned out and began the search. Eventually they found an elderly man, too infirmed to leave his bed. After ascertaining he was in his late 60s, Henderson ordered the helpless man shot. He was under 70, so the order was strictly applied.

After the Argyll's had ensured that no living MacDonald were alive, the troops were ordered to strip the village of all property and livestock left behind. It included twelve hundred head of cattle and horse, plus a quantity of goats and sheep. These were herded to the regimental garrison at Fort William and later divided among the Garrison. Undoubtedly, many were the result of inter clan feuds, and some of these were formerly Campbell's livestock.

Some 7 miles from the village, and safe in the mountains, Annella was coming to terms with the loss of her world. She had no way of knowing how many had survived. Here in the small community of Kinlochmore in the mountains, overlooking Loch Leven, there were around 30 survivors, among them were Maclain's two sons and their families. Between them and Glencoe, many lay buried in the snow. Their bodies would not be found until the snow melted, and even then, in the higher elevations they would remain lost for months.

During the morning, more survivors stumbled into the relative sanctuary of the settlement. Some had grim tales to tell, women told of husbands who pleaded with the soldiers whom they had befriended, even as they were being shot down.

Mothers told of young babies dying in their arms as they fled into the freezing night. Worst of all, was the children who survived, wandering aimlessly with blank expressions, as if to try and make sense of what they had just witnessed.

Annella was fearful when she heard that John and his brothers were planning to return to Glencoe the following day. To recover bodies, and to ensure the dead, including their father, received a decent burial. However, John was sure that the soldiers would have long gone, taking the cattle and property with them.

There was no shelter left in the village and the soldiers would not wish to camp out in this charnel house of death. In this, his instincts proved correct.

As he and his party approached the village, it seemed totally deserted. Carefully, he watched for an hour, for any sign of a rear guard or sentry, but there were none. John, who now was the rightful successor to the Maclains of The Clan MacDonald of Glencoe, took no chances. He posted men at the end of the street, affording a good view of the road to Fort William. He also scanned the isle of Eileen Munde, just offshore in the Loch through his spyglass. This was the family burial ground of the Clan, and he was aware that Campbell also knew this. It was more than possible that he had men there waiting for John to bring the body over for burial.

At the Chief's burned-out house, he found the body of his father and servants in the ruins; they had been burned, but he was still recognisable. His mother's naked body lay frozen in death, her eyes wide open, staring at the morning sky. Carefully, they wrapped the bodies in makeshift shrouds and bound them with rope.

There was still a cold mist on the loch and around the lower shore of the island.

John secured a longboat and put several men aboard to scout the island and prepare the graves. After an hour, he saw the all clear wave from the party, and by mid- afternoon the first bodies were being rowed across the loch.

Alexander and his wife were the first to be buried on a high bluff looking back towards Glencoe. It seemed fitting that the spirit of the old chief would be able to watch over his people for eternity. John and his brother, as well as Jean Campbell's niece, stood silently as John read over the graves. Other bodies were being prepared as more survivors drifted back from the mountains. They did not include any children, and only a few widows.

By the fourth day, the guard at the entrance to the village reported a rider approaching from fort William, and he was dressed in non-military winter clothing.

As he entered the street, he saw John and his brothers standing in his path and blocking the way. He stopped about 10 yards away and dismounted.

"Sir, I am looking for John Maclain, the son of Alexander. The late Laird of Glencoe. Can you take me to him? I have urgent business to discuss."

John looked the man up and down; he was well wrapped but still seemed very cold.

"And who may you be, sir, to come seeking the new Chief, so soon after the foul murder of my Father? Ye dinna have the look of a soldier, maybe a peddler."

The comment drew laughter from the clansmen.

The stranger looked awkward and unsure of how to answer; these highlanders looked very dangerous.

"I assure you, sir, I am not in the military, nor do I want to sell you anything. I am here at the request of My Lord Breadalbane, with a message for the new chief. May I assume that man be yourself, sir?"

John's smile faded at the mention of Breadalbane's name, but was interested enough to hear the man out.

"I am John Maclain; what does that treacherous Campbell of Breadalbane want of me? For my part, I will settle for his head. And that of Robert Campbell to boot."

There was a murmur of approval from John's companions.

The messenger continued.

"My Lord Breadalbane feels you and your people suffered a great wrong. He assures you he had no knowledge of what the Army was planning. Although he cannot undo the grievous injustice done to you, he wishes you well, and in return for a letter signed by you, that he had no part in the great wrong done to your people. He will offer his protection and petition the King to have your rights and lands restored to you."

John, of course, was well aware that Breadalbane was one of the instigators of the massacre. However, he resisted rejecting the offer out of hand. He realised the only reason the offer was being made was that, with so many witnesses, Breadalbane was vulnerable. Also, as a leading member of the Privy Council, he would be in a position to protect the survivors and could indeed be influential in obtaining a king's pardon. John bade the messenger to sit with the survivors, in the partial shelter of a burned out house, while they questioned him further.

Meanwhile, in a tavern in Edinburgh, over 100 miles from the devastation at Glencoe, a Redcoat officer was slumped in a chair with a half empty bottle of whisky on the table in front of him.

Captain Robert Campbell was drunk, but not drunk enough to erase the memories of the past week. Every time he closed his eyes, he saw again the face of the pleading youth, with blood bubbling from his mouth. He heard the anguished cries of mothers who had seen their families slaughtered in front of them, the smell of burning wood smoke and black powder, and the distant crack of rifle fire. This was no righteous battle. There was no honour in slaughtering women, children, and infants who had treated the redcoats as guests. He kept telling himself that he had done as ordered and had the written proof in his pocket. However, unbeknownst to him, that was no longer the case. In a fit of coughing, he had pulled his neckerchief from his pocket, dislodging the folded order, which now lay on the tavern floor. Other soldiers in the tavern were keeping their distance. All knew it would be unwise to approach him in this mood, and some who had been with him at Glencoe knew too well the demons that were tormenting his mind. They too had nightmares.

Finally, he got to his feet and stumbled out of the door. Most were relieved to see him go. Later, after the bar closed, a serving girl noticed the folded note, and unable to read, handed it to the tavern keeper. Unfortunately for Campbell, this classified document was now in the hands of a man who could not only read, but who was also no friend of the King. A Jacobite sympathiser, he made arrangements for the order to be sent to France, where King James still held court. Within days, it appeared in a Paris newspaper, along with an account of the massacre by King Williams's men.

A few days later, word arrived at Glencoe that Breadalbane had kept his word in the form of a letter from the Privy Council, granting full protection to the survivors, and confirming that a petition had been sent to the King requesting full clemency in the form of a royal pardon. Slowly, the survivors returned to their ravaged hamlets and began the act of rebuilding their homes.

In the following days, shock and horror of the massacre spread through the highlands. Not because of the raid itself. Such incidents were common enough in Scotland. However, murder under trust and the absolute betrayal of Highland hospitality was too

For his part, Secretary Dalrymple had no regrets, save that he publically announced that he regretted some MacDonalds had escaped the massacre. He was confident that the destruction of Glencoe and the removal of all livestock would ensure that the clan never returned. So sanctimonious was he, that he had little concept of the wave of revulsion being aimed squarely at him by most of the Highland clans. But while Dalrymple considered himself untouchable, Breadalbane was a very worried man. He had anticipated that the entire clan would be slaughtered, and there would be no witnesses. The fact that many had escaped, and an enquiry had been ordered, meant that he would have difficulty in avoiding blame. This was why he had made the offer to the Heir apparent to the Clan.

The Privy Council also was aware that they served only at the pleasure of the king. They had all quickly agreed to try to undo the damage.

However Breadalbane was not out of the woods yet. Someone discovered the document pledging to reverse the Clan's allegiance and brought it to the attention of King William.

With the Clans brought to heel, and the Jacobites scattered, their King in Exile in France; William should have been well satisfied. However, word had reached him of the incident at Glencoe, and a rising well of anger directed at him from north of the border. He had summoned his lord chancellor for an explanation.

As usual, at these times, his wife Mary was on hand to cool tempers. The Chancellor, John Somers, had anticipated the reason for the summons and was holding a copy of the order signed by the King.

Quickly, the Chancellor, John Somers, outlined the circumstances of the massacre and the authority for it, with an order signed by his majesty. William took the order and read it before commenting.

"I sign many such orders every day, my lord. Can you expect me to read every one? This is why we rely on good advisors. Now I hear from Scotland, that I am being accused of cold blooded murder. Why was I not informed that these clansmen had signed the pledge late, and why was the petition not passed to me for consideration? Is not that the clear intent of this order?"

Somers felt decidedly uncomfortable, but had no intention of taking the fall for highland incompetence.

"Indeed, my lord, you are most correct. From my understanding, the problem is My Lord Breadalbane. Who it appears has a personal grudge against the MacDonalds. It would seem that he used your majesty's order to try to eliminate the clan. I have not, as yet, been able to determine the full facts as to why the petition details were not passed to the crown."

William nodded.

"This makes sense. In truth, it has been brought to my attention that Breadalbane has been in contact with my wife's brother, and expressed a promise to pledge allegiance to him, should James mount an invasion. Today I received a petition from him, pleading for clemency for the MacDonald's, who survived. It would seem that the Lord Breadalbane is a dog that serves two masters. It is my order that Lord Breadalbane be placed under arrest on a charge of high treason, to await my pleasure."

Somers bowed and took his leave. The king now turned to Mary.

"It seems the Highlanders of Scotland are going to be a continuing problem for our person. They are constantly warring amid themselves and have no compulsion in shedding blood. Now we hear they blame me for the bloodshed. Tell me my Queen, what would your advice be to our person?"

Mary expected the question, but hesitated before replying.

"My Lord, the Scots are a wild and unpredictable race. However, they do have a strong sense of honour. The accounts of this affair are most disturbing, in that the soldiers stayed with the families of the Macdonald's for two weeks before falling upon them. To the Scots, this is an unforgivable crime. They deem Murder under Trust. They may criticise you, my Lord over the order, but I fear the Clan Campbell will bear the responsibility. My advice would be to order a full enquiry and punish those who mislead you. Breadalbane, of course, but I feel the Scottish Privy Council did not serve you well."

The King smiled and took Mary's hand. He smiled, but did not reply, leaving her unsure of whether her husband would follow her advice.

Chapter 13

Consequences

Francis Farquhar and Gilbert Kennedy were confined to quarters at Fort William. Pending their court martial, they were held under guard; and as the weeks went by, were becoming increasingly depressed. McBane was in Holland with the regiment. The rumour was, he got drunk while escorting recruits and ended up on the ship transporting them. Gilbert was glad he was not here. The two junior officers had no idea of the fate of Annella, but had heard the operation had not gone according to plan, that less than half of the clansmen had been killed, and that questions were already being asked being asked.

It was no real surprise when a major from the Regiment arrived to interview them. What was a surprise was he was not alone. A member of the Scottish Privy Council accompanied him. The Major and his companion drew up chairs and set them in front of a long oak dining table. Then the Major spoke.

"Gentlemen, please sit down. We have a proposition to put to you."

The two friends looked surprised, but quickly complied. The Civilian spoke first.

"I am here from the Scottish Privy Council, to ask you about the unfortunate events at Glencoe. The King has directed us to carry out a full enquiry into this matter. If you agree to assist us fully in that enterprise and testify to the council, we are prepared to drop the charges against you."

The young officers looked at each other in disbelief. This sounded a little too perfect.

The Major then interjected.

"Gentlemen, I advise you to consider this offer seriously. Disobedience of orders during a military operation is a very grave offense."

Gilbert spoke first.

"For my part, sir, I have no regrets for refusing to carry out this order. I will fight the enemies of the King as I have sworn, but will not slaughter

helpless women and children who have come to trust me. I would willingly testify to the horrors I witnessed."

Francis nodded. *"I agree with Lt Kennedy on this point, sir. May I ask if you intend to question Captain Campbell and Major Duncanson on the matter, sir? Our understanding was the order was issued to Captain Campbell, from the Major."*

The Privy councillor answered truthfully.

"We are indeed, Lieutenant. I can tell you that the Lord Breadalbane has been arrested on the orders of the King, and we at the council have suspended the order allowing the attack on the Clan Macdonald. The survivors are returning to the glen under the protection of the King. So can I take it from your answers you accept the Council's terms?"

Francis smiled to himself. In truth, he would happily have testified without any deal. But he took the Councillor's hand, as did Digby.

The Major stood up and addressed the two men.

"Thank you gentlemen, the charges against you are hereby dismissed."

He smiled and continued,

"May I add it is a serious matter to disobey orders in the field, and only in extraordinary circumstances can it be justified. I believe that these are such circumstances. I feel your actions have done credit to you and your regiment. You are free to resume your duties."

****

Two weeks after the massacre, Francis and Gilbert decided they had to find out the fate of Annella; they owed it to McBane, and had already waited too long. The trip would be dangerous, and feelings were still running high in Glencoe, but the truce had held, and Francis felt it unlikely that the MacDonalds would break it.

With that in mind, the two redcoats set out for the village. The weather had improved and their journey was unimpeded, reaching the glen without a problem. The residents payed them little heed until they had travelled about a mile.

They rode slowly between the ruined houses, noting that repairs were already well underway. Even after the passage of time, the smell of burnt - wet wood hung in the air. The icy stares from the villagers were like knives cutting through them. One woman spat at them as they passed, shouting, "Bastards!"

However, there was no hostile action.

Francis scanned the gaunt faces, looking for Annella, but failing to see her. He began to fear the worst, and then he saw a familiar face among the MacDonalds. Alexander's son, John, put down the bucket of creek stones he was taking to a re-construction and approached them.

"I recognise you two. You are the men that refused to take part in the murders here. For that, I thank you. But I fear the sentiments will nae be shared by my highlanders."

Francis nodded understandingly.

"This was a great wrong done to you and your people, John, there's no denying it. There is justice, for knowing the King has vowed to root out those responsible."

John was hardly gladdened by the news.

"Well, if the king needs to place blame, then he need look no further than the signature on the order. You as soldiers just obey orders, isn't that right?"

Francis knew he spoke the truth, but it was Gilbert who replied.

"Not always John, some of us have been known to, shall we say, disagree?"

"Touché"

The remark startled them. Francis turned quickly to see Annella, who had approached unseen from an almost repaired hut. Her remark seemed puzzling to all but the two officers. She at least seemed pleased to see them.

Francis quickly dismounted and embraced her.

"Thank God you're safe Lassie."

"Thank God, maybe; but first, I really need to thank Lieutenant Francis Farquhar of the Kings Argyll's regiment of foot."

She extended her hand, and Francis gratefully took it.

He spoke softly to her.

"Miss MacDonald, it is to my lasting regret that we were unable to save more of your people. I hope it will be of some comfort to you, that the men who planned and ordered the attack will face full justice."

Annella turned away with an almost incredulous smile before turning back to him.

"And that justice will extend to your king, will it, Francis?"

The words were cutting, but nevertheless, true. Francis now noted the sudden interest in their conversation. He would have to choose his words of reply carefully.

"The King is far away from Glencoe, in London. He has to rely on advice from his Lord Chancellor and his Privy Council. It would appear that he was given false information by them to settle a land dispute. The Lord Breadalbane has already been arrested on that count. And whether or not you see him as your king is a moot point. He reigns over this Kingdom, including Scotland."

Annella thought momentarily before replying.

"James is our King, and always will be, here in the fair highlands of our bonnie Glen. William cannot command loyalty; he will have to earn it."

A chorus of assent went up from the assembled group.

"This is a bad time for my people, and there will be anger and grief for many years, Francis. In time, those scars may heal, but for now, let us just say, we need time to heal and time to rebuild. Farewell soldier, keep ye safe, and may the good Lord look kindly to you, and to Donald."

Gilbert and Francis nodded, and remounted their horses before riding slowly out of the Glen. They never saw Annella again, nor did they remain at Fort William. In accordance with the desire to separate the redcoats that took part in the Massacre, the regiment was posted out to Europe, and the events at Glencoe were passed into history. Except in the highlands, where the memories still burn with a light to rival any found in a Highland crofts, warming winter blaze.

The End

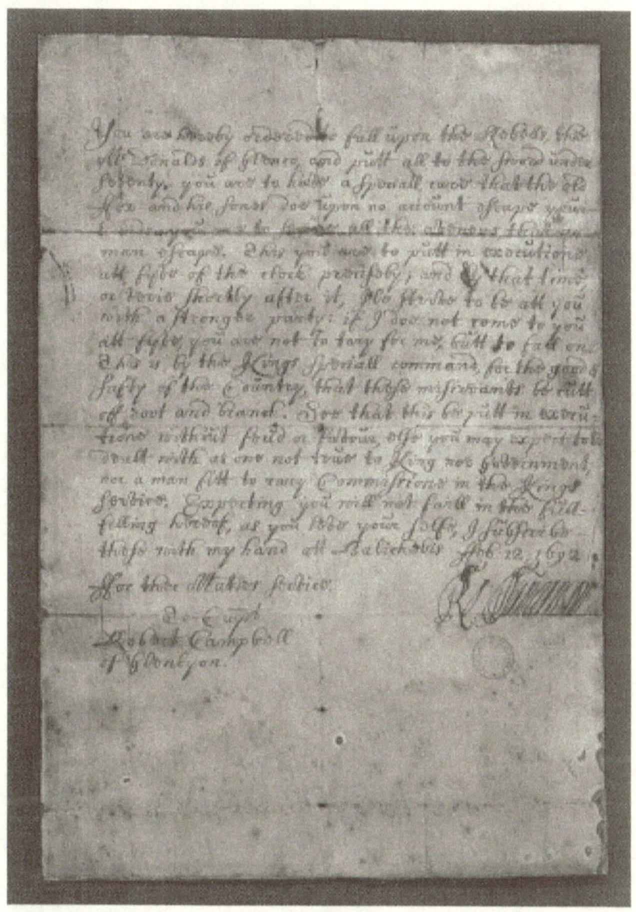

The original order to Captain Robert Campbell, ordering the Massacre.

Soldiers Leap at Killiecrankie Pass, the site of Donald Mcbane's legendary leap.

Highlanders under the command of John Claverhouse, Earl of Dundee (Bonnie Dundee), try to surround and capture British Commander General Mackay during the disastrous engagement at Killiecrankie Pass.

91

Biographies

Archibald Campbell, 10th Earl, and 1st Duke of Argyll

Archibald Campbell, 10th Earl, and 1st Duke of Argyll, was born in 1651 at Cheriton House, England and died on September 25th 1705. He was Chief of the Clan Campbell and took part in the 'Glorious Revolution' from 1688 to 1689. He was a powerful supporter of William of Orange, and in 1689, was admitted to the Convention of the Scottish Estates, as the Earl of Argyll. Deputed with Sir James Montgomery and Sir John Dalrymple in its name, and to present the crown and administer the oath to King William the 3rd on his coronation. Widely regarded as the architect of the Massacre of Glencoe, Archibald Campbell was shunned by the Scottish Highlanders as being guilty of the most heinous crime in Scotland, that of 'Murder under Trust'.

CRUEL IS THE SNOW

Captain Robert Campbell

Captain Robert Campbell of Glenlyon was Commander of the Argyll's Company of Foot that carried out the Massacre of Glencoe, following the order given to him by his commanding officer, Lt Col Hamilton, under the authority of King William 3rd. Glenlyon was chosen for the mission primarily because he was a Campbell and had a grievance against the Macdonald men. John Dalrymple was a shrewd man and needed a scapegoat in case questions were asked. The unwitting captain was such a man. Robert and his 120 redcoat soldiers duly arrived at Glencoe on 1st February, ostensibly on a tax collecting mission and were hospitably received by the Maclain's people. Campbell had been a frequent visitor at the village, due to his relationship to the Maclains through marriage of his niece to John Maclain, the Chief's son. And at 5 am on the morning of 13th February, they rose against their unsuspecting hosts and began to slaughter them. In the dark and the confusion many escaped, leaving Glenlyon with but 38 corpses to show for his night's work. Following the massacre, the officer bore the brunt of the blame for the incident and began drinking heavily. He was posted to Flanders with his regiment, with the majority of the men involved in the massacre. Following the defeat of the regiment at the 'Battle of Diksmuide' in 1696, the mentally broken officer died, drunk and in a gutter, on the streets of Bruges, later the same year.

CRUEL IS THE SNOW

Donald McBane

Portrait of Donald McBane, Scottish Fencing Master, from his own
book "The Expert Swordsman's Companion"

Following his much celebrated leap over the Burn at Killiecrankie pass, McBane remained in the army of King William, stationed mostly at Fort William. He was not present at the massacre, being in Europe at the time, after inexplicably being mistakenly taken to France with a party of recruits that he was supposed to be escorting to the ferry a few weeks after the event.

McBane took fencing lessons early in his service and became a master swordsman, teaching his skills to his military colleagues. He later wrote a book, '*The Master Swordsman*,' which became a bestseller, illustrating the finer points of swordsmanship.

The book, still in print today, and is a testament to the finer points of warfare in the 16th century.

John Dalrymple

John Dalrymple (1648 - 1707) was the architect of the Treaty of Union between Scotland and England that created the Kingdom of Great Britain.

The son of James Dalrymple, 1st Viscount of Stair, John Dalrymple, was born at Stair House in the parish of Stair, in Kyle Ayrshire. He served under King James, but as a dominant force in the Scottish Parliament, he helped bring about the accession of William 2nd of Scotland. The king rewarded him with the position of Lord Advocate, and in 1691, was appointed Joint Secretary of State over Scotland with James Johnson.

Dalrymple is most remembered for his part in the 1692 Massacre of Glencoe. In 1695, the Scottish parliament demanded an enquiry into the massacre, and when the report from the enquiry was complete, they voted that "the killing of the Glencoe men was murder."

Responsibility for the crime lay with the King's Scottish ministers, and many criticised Williams shielding the Master of Stair. The only punishment he endured was a dismissal from the Secretaryship of State. He returned to the government in 1700 as a member of the Privy Council of Scotland. After succeeding his father as 2nd Viscount of Stair, in 1695, he was created 1st Earl of Stair in 1703, by Queen Ann.

King William 3rd Prince of Orange

King William of Orange was a divisive monarch, both in England and Scotland. He was invited to succeed to the crown by the British Parliament. William, a prince of Orange, married Princess Mary, the Daughter of Charles 1st. This was a marriage of convenience and helped the English people to accept him as monarch. On landing in England with his army, on November the fifth, the king noted celebrations were in place already, and was told that the date was significant to the English for another reason as it marked the deliverance of King James, from an assassination attempt 83 years earlier that was known as the gunpowder plot. William, possibly on the advice of his wife, decreed that the date would also mark his arrival and deliverance of the English from James 2nd. William and his wife Mary were crowned joint monarchs of England, Scotland, and Ireland in 1689. Their accession, known as the 'Glorious Revolution', marked an important transition towards parliamentary rule as we know it today. William's ousting of his predecessor, the Catholic James II, ensured the primacy of the Protestant faith in Britain. His decisive victory over James at the Battle of the Boyne is celebrated annually in Northern Ireland on 12 July. In Europe, William was successful in his lifelong struggle to contain the military ambitions of Louis XIV, the Catholic king of France. In part to help finance his wars with Louis, William also founded the Bank of England.

Queen Mary 2nd

Although her father and mother were converts to the Roman Catholic faith, Mary was brought up a Protestant. In November 1677, she was married to her cousin William of Orange, and champion of the Protestant cause in Europe. She then settled in Holland. Her inability to bear children, and William's infidelity, made the early years of her marriage unhappy, but eventually they became a devoted couple.

During the quarrel (1687–88) between James II and William over James's pro-Catholic policies, Mary felt it her religious duty to side with her husband. Hence, she agreed to support William's invasion of England in November 1688. James fled the country in December, and two months later, Mary arrived in London. At once Mary rejected proposals, advanced particularly by the Earl of Danby, that she become sole ruler to the exclusion of her husband, and on April 11, 1689, she and William were crowned joint Sovereigns of England, Scotland, and Ireland. While her husband was directing military campaigns in Ireland and on the Continent, Mary administered the government in her own name, but she relied entirely on his advice. In the periods when William was in England, she willingly retired from politics. Mary was a popular choice of the people until her death from Smallpox at the age of 32.

Alasdair Ruadh MacIain MacDonald, 12th Laird of Glencoe
(No Photo Available)

Until his untimely death, Alasdair Macdonald was the Chief of the Maclain sept of the Glencoe branch of the MacDonalds clan, usually referred to as The MacDonalds of Glencoe. The Clan had been a thorn in the side of the Privy Council for many years, and Alasdair had orchestrated many raids against the Clan Campbell, who occupied lands they felt were rightfully theirs. The British Garrison at Fort William was aware of the situation, but was unable to gather sufficient evidence to bring charges. This led the Clan Chief to be dubbed 'The Old Fox' by the authorities.

Alasdair was certainly no saint and was guilty of much banditry in the region at that time. There is little doubt that the order from King William gave the Campbell clan the opportunity to eradicate the Clan once and for all. This was encouraged by the British authorities. However, it should be noted that few of the redcoat soldiers who carried out the massacre were Campbells.

KING James the Second

The man who became King James the second was born James Stuart, on October 14, 1633, at St. James's Palace in London. He was the third son of King Charles I, and of his wife, Princess Henrietta Maria of France. From his birth, James bore the title of "Prince of England, Scotland, France, and Ireland." At the same time, he was designated "Duke of York."

In 1638, James was named Lord High Admiral of England. He was named a Knight of the 'Most Noble Order of the Garter', April 20, 1642, and raised to the Peerage of England with the title of 'Duke of York' on January 27, 1644.

At the death of his brother Charles II, February 6, 1685, James succeeded as king. He was crowned privately, according to the rites of the Catholic Church on April 22, 1685, at Whitehall Palace, and publicly according to the rites of the Church of England, April 23, 1685, at Westminster Abbey.

However, there were many in England who felt that his recent conversion to the Catholic faith was a sham to legitimise his claim to the throne. This split the church and led no less than 5 English peers, and two commoners on June 20th, 1688 to petition Prince William of Orange, James's son in law, to invade England by force and reclaim the Throne. William was married to Charles 1st daughter, Mary, who made the choice more acceptable to the British people. William landed in England at the head of a large army and was greeted warmly by the local populace. He chose November 5th, 1688, as it was a significant date in the English calendar commemorating the thwarting of the assassination of James 1st, during what was known as the Gunpowder Plot. James refused to engage Williams's army and fled to France in exile.

James died September 16, 1701, at the Chateau of St Germaine en Laye, never having returned to England. His son James succeeded him in all his British rights. James was, however, not destined to rest in peace. His body was put in a coffin, and left unburied, in the Chapel of Saint Edmund in the Church of the English Benedictines, in the Rue St. Jacques, Paris.

His brain was sent to the Scots College in Paris, his heart to the Convent of the Visitandine Nuns at Chaillot, and his bowels divided between the English Church of St. Omer and the parish church of St. Germain-en-Laye. James' body remained in the Church of the English Benedictines, waiting transportation to Westminster Abbey, until the French Revolution, where it was desecrated by the mob and lost.

CRUEL IS THE SNOW

Authors Note

The massacre of Glencoe echoes down through the years as one of the most heinous acts ever committed by a government on its people. It ranks, in my opinion, alongside the Trail of Tears, the massacre at Wounded Knee and the mass incarceration of American Asian citizens during WW2. This is not because of the body count or the overwhelming firepower used. In Scotland, the people have a streak of patriotism that was too often ignored by the monarchy and the religious leadership of England. It was because the murderers were guests of their victims who trusted them and formed friendships over the two weeks prior to the attack.

The country has a long history of resistance to any concept of rule by the English Parliament. It has its own laws and customs. And fiercely opposes all efforts to fully integrate with the rest of the kingdom. One law in particular is considered so heinous that it carries a penalty far beyond the original perpetrator. Commission of this offence will incur shame and punishment not only on the original perpetrator but also his family and their descendants. That Crime is Murder under Trust, the massacre of Glencoe, was just such a crime. Even today Glencoe and the Fort William area you can see signs saying 'Campbells not welcome' in various retail establishments, particularly cafes and the odd bar. Time is, of course, a great healer on many fronts. A few years back, I attended a Burns Night event in hosted by The Scottish Society of Louisville. I had just finished the first edition of Cruel is the snow and had taken some copies both to sell and as door prizes.

One of the dignitaries present was a certain Colonel Campbell, resplendent in his mess dress. His wife accompanied him and introduced herself as a member of the Clan McDonald, and wore the appropriate tartan skirt and plaid. In their case, there was obviously no animosity. But I could not help but wonder if they were the exception or the rule.

In this edition, I have delved deep into the events of that night, reading eyewitness testimony and consulting official records. The relationship between Annella and McBane is fictional, of course, and included for dramatic effect, but the events described are documented and the people real.

Laird Stephen C. Challis (Rank acquired 2024)

About the Author

Steve Challis was born in 1948 in the United Kingdom. Steve grew up in the rural Cotswold's where he learned shooting and hunting on the farm where his Father worked. Following 5 years of service in the military (RAF), Steve joined the Hampshire Constabulary in 1969 and served as an officer for 21 years. In 2006, Steve met his wife Eva via the internet, and then in 2007 they became engaged. The following year in November, Steve moved to the USA and he and Eva were married in Ketchikan, Alaska. Now a permanent US resident, Steve is the author of several books on gun rights and historical fiction.